To Jacob

Enjoy the mystery

Sheila McIntyre

# THE CAVE
## IN THE
# FOREST

### SHEILA ADAM MCINTYRE

ISBN 978-0-7414-7480-3

Printed in the United States of America

Published April 2012

INFINITY PUBLISHING
1094 New DeHaven Street, Suite 100
West Conshohocken, PA 19428-2713
Toll-free (877) BUY BOOK
Local Phone (610) 941-9999
Fax (610) 941-9959
Info@buybooksontheweb.com
www.buybooksontheweb.com

# TABLE OF CONTENTS

# CHAPTER 1

## A MYSTERIOUS EVENT

The sun was just beginning to disappear behind the trees in the Great National Forest when thirteen-year-old Jonathan Taylor and his best friend, Buzz Cameron, stopped their bicycles by the split rail fence at the side of the road. The darkening forms of the trees were becoming a threatening jungle of spooky shapes.

"That's one scary looking place," Jonathan frowned. "I wouldn't be dumb enough to go in there right now even if you paid me."

"Yeah, I know what you mean. What if something was hiding behind those trees?"

"Lots of people in Jacobsville won't go anywhere near the place, even in daylight," Jonathan said. "They swear they've seen ghosts and that some hunters have even disappeared."

"Do you believe all that stuff?"

Jonathan paused to think. "I'm not sure, especially about the ghosts."

Buzz slowly nodded his head. "Yeah, ghosts are some-thing else. You just never know for sure about them."

"Whenever we went fishing at that lake in the forest, nothing happened," Jonathan pointed out. "It was always sunny and bright."

"I know. You just have to be sure you're out of there before dark," Buzz warned.

They got back on their bikes and pushed off. When they got as far as Jonathan's house he stopped.

"Buzz, did you know there's a cave in the forest?"

"No kidding!"

"It's true. A teacher said that one time. She said it's only a mile west of the lake."

"How come I never heard of that before?" Buzz asked.

"I guess it's because those people in town are so spooked they won't even talk about anything to do with the place. And get this, she said people who explore caves are called spelunkers."

"Sp-spelunkers?" Buzz laughed.

"I know. It sounds weird. She even showed us a video. All the spelunkers wore helmets with lights attached. It must be real dark in there."

"What if there are drawings on the cave walls and bones and stuff? I saw that on a program about a cave in Egypt." Buzz said.

"Maybe there are. We should check it out. Let's go tomorrow morning." Jonathan turned his bike onto the driveway.

"Well, maybe. I guess we could," Buzz said with some hesitation.

"Nothing's going to happen to us," Jonathan insisted. "Let's meet at the forest entrance at ten o'clock. We'd better bring flashlights."

The next morning, they met as planned. They hid their bikes behind a clump of bushes, and began to walk toward the lake. A chorus of small birds twittered in the treetops.

Suddenly, something appeared in the sky that was so large it blocked the sun, causing the forest to darken. Jonathan pushed his straight, black hair out of his eyes as he looked up to try and identify it through the treetops, but it was too dark to see anything. As it moved along, the object created a swishing sound barely loud enough to be heard. Then it appeared to stop, hovering directly above them in complete silence. Both boys stood frozen, almost afraid to breathe. Jonathan thought his heart might jump right out of his chest. When the swishing sound returned, it gradually became weaker as the object slowly moved away, allowing the sun to shine through the treetops again. But the twittering birds had become silent as if in fear, and a strange stillness filled the air.

"W-what was that?" Buzz whispered.

Jonathan didn't know what to think. "Maybe it's some sort of gigantic bird or something."

"How could a bird be that big?"

"I don't know," Jonathan's eyes widened. "What if it's a spaceship?"

"I hope it's not." Buzz's face turned pale with fear. "Shouldn't we go home, right now? We can always come back."

Jonathan could feel himself shaking inside. *What if the thing did come back?* "Okay, let's get out of here."

They had just returned to their bikes when Jonathan stopped. "You know what, Buzz? We definitely need to come back so we won't chicken out, or we might never find out what that shadow was. It's gone now. Anyway, we still need to look for the cave."

Buzz tried to convince himself. "I guess we should."

"We'll just be real careful," Jonathan assured him. "How about we meet again tomorrow morning at nine o'clock? That'll give us plenty of time."

"Well, okay," Buzz agreed. Still feeling a bit uneasy, he turned to look back above the trees, but there was no sign of the object.

They took off for home.

# CHAPTER 2

## A QUESTION OF TIME

The next morning, Jonathan woke up just as his mother was leaving for work at the local hospital.

"Jonathan," she called upstairs, "I forgot to tell you I'll be working overtime today. I won't be home until around eight-thirty. I'll grab something to eat in the cafeteria. There's some leftover chicken and rice casserole in the fridge. You can heat it up for dinner."

"Okay, Mom, thanks."

"Could you please mow the lawn this morning?" she asked. "It's getting way too long."

"Sure, Mom. I'll do it right after breakfast."

After his mother left, Jonathan got dressed and went downstairs to the kitchen to phone Buzz.

"I have to cut the lawn before I leave. How about we meet at ten? And let's bring a sandwich, or something." He listened for a moment then smiled. "That's cool. See you." He hung up the phone and poured some cereal into a bowl, added milk and wolfed it down. Then he made a peanut butter and jelly sandwich for his lunch. He put it in his backpack, along with a box of apple juice and the flashlight, then went to the garage to get the lawnmower.

Jonathan was so excited about his planned adventure that he finished the job quickly and was soon on his way to the forest.

When they met, they hid their bikes as before, put on their backpacks and set off.

"I wonder if that big thing, whatever it was, will come back," Jonathan said. "I hope not."

As they walked past the lake they kept looking up at the sky, but the mysterious object was nowhere to be seen. They continued along the narrow pathway beside the river that flowed from the lake.

"Now, we need to go a mile west of the lake," Jonathan said.

"Which way is west?" asked Buzz.

"Well, I remember hearing that the sun rises in the east and sets in the west. This is the direction it goes down, so we're going the right way."

"I hope we don't get lost," Buzz frowned.

"I thought about that. So to make sure it won't happen, I cut up a ton of red string I found in the basement." Jonathan reached into his backpack, pulled out a handful and gave some to Buzz. "We can tie it on some of the bushes to mark our path so we can find our way back."

They kept on walking, carefully attaching the pieces of string as they went. "We're like real explorers," Jonathan grinned.

They seemed to have gone a fair distance when they came to what looked like a pile of large rocks arranged in such a way that they formed an opening.

"Could that be the cave?" Jonathan said excitedly.

They approached it slowly. When they reached the opening, Jonathan got down on his knees to peer inside.

"This hole looks so small."

"Do you think we can squeeze in there?" Buzz asked.

"Let me shine the light inside and see what it looks like." Jonathan took the flashlight out of his backpack and lay down flat on his stomach. He shone the light through the opening. "Wow! Buzz, have a look at this." He moved aside.

Buzz took out his own flashlight, got down and aimed the light beam inside. "This is way cool! The bottom goes pretty far down, and it looks like a humungous underground cave just like that one I saw on TV."

"Move over and let me have another look." Jonathan studied the area for a moment. "There's a big ledge to stand on just inside and some flat rocks to climb down on. I'm sure we can get through here."

"Well, yeah, I'm sure you can fit in there," Buzz said. "You're pretty skinny."

"Let's try it." Jonathan put his flashlight in his pocket. "I'll go first. Keep shining your light from way at the side so I won't block it when I slide through."

Buzz held onto the light tightly as Jonathan pulled himself through the opening. "It's real easy," he called up. "The ledge is right there where you can stand up. And the stones are kind of like going down stairs." His voice sounded distant and created a sort of echo. "Buzz, push our backpacks down."

But, Buzz didn't seem too sure about this whole plan. "Are you positive we'll be able to get back out?" he asked in a quavering voice.

"Sure, no problem." Jonathan's echo sounded very confident. "We can easily climb back up on the rocks and that ledge."

Slowly, Buzz ran his hands through his disheveled mass of brown hair as he stood there staring at the small entrance trying to work up his courage. "Okay, if I can get through, I'm coming down. I'll try." He pushed both backpacks through the opening sending them crashing down.

Buzz held the flashlight tightly in his hand. He worked at pulling himself through the hole while twisting and turning his body. Suddenly, he was propelled to the other side like a cork popping out of a bottle and landed on the ledge.

"Wow! This is awesome," he said. "I've never even seen a picture of a cave like this before, ever." He climbed down the flat rocks until he reached the cave floor. "Doesn't it feel colder down here?"

"Yeah. It's like a breeze blowing, or something." It's sort of damp, too. Do you hear water dripping?"

Buzz stood quietly to listen. "I think I do."

"Let's go in a little farther," Jonathan turned and began to walk carefully over the uneven floor of the cave.

"Okay," Buzz said. "But should we put down pieces of string here too?"

"No, I don't think we'll need them. We'll just go around the corner up ahead and check it out. That's all."

They followed the beam of the flashlight being very careful not to trip. When they turned the corner, the cave opened up into a huge grotto as the ground sloped downwards.

Jonathan shone his light up at the ceiling. "See those spiky things hanging down? They're called stalactites. They're made when water drips down that dissolves some of the limestone. Each drop leaves crystals on the ceiling that keep growing. I learned that from the teacher."

"Cool, that's so neat," Buzz said as he followed the beam of the flashlight.

Jonathan continued. "See those coming up from the floor of the cave? They're called stalagmites from a build-up of the crystals from the bottom."

"Wow!" Buzz looked all around him at the oddly shaped forms. "That's so awesome."

"Let's sit here on this flat formation and look around." They plopped their backpacks on the ground and sat down. "Look, we can even lean back." They shone their flashlights on the ceiling and at all the strange shapes, causing them to sparkle like stars.

"Echo!" Jonathan shouted as loud as he could. The sound reverberated, bouncing off the walls as it got more and more faint and finally disappeared.

"That's so cool." Buzz cupped his mouth with his hands and shouted even louder. "Hello!" Once again the sound bounced around until it could no longer be heard.

Suddenly, Jonathan sat up very straight. "Buzz, did you hear that funny noise just now?"

"Yeah, I think I heard something."

"It sounded a lot like whispering, or like the swishing sound we heard when that big thing went overhead yesterday." Jonathan sat very still to listen. "What if it's hovering right above us?"

"Do you want to go back outside to look?" Buzz asked.

"I don't think so. What if it sees us? We'd better stay where we are. Anyway, if it is that same thing, it'll be going in a minute or two, like it did yesterday." He tried to convince himself. "That sound could have been just the wind or something."

"Yeah, I think that's what the wind would sound like from inside a cave," Buzz said, trying to calm his own nerves. "I don't hear it now anyway. If it was up there, it's gone."

"Okay. Let's turn off the flashlights and just sit quietly. Maybe there are eerie sounds in caves because of all the formations and the air flowing around them."

It seemed to Jonathan like a few minutes later when he stood up. He turned on his flashlight. "I think my batteries must be getting kind of weak. We both need a good light. Let's go outside. We can come back another day and do some real exploring."

They returned to the entrance and pushed their backpacks ahead of them as they climbed up the rocks to the ledge. Jonathan worked his way through the opening first and stood up. It was getting dark outside. He called back to Buzz. "This is crazy! The sun's going down."

Buzz followed, squeezing his way through the opening. "What's going on here? It can't be that late."

"I know," Jonathan said.

Buzz looked all around him. "Isn't it early afternoon?"

"I think so. I didn't bring my watch. Maybe that big thing, whatever it was, really did come back."

"What if it did something to us, like put us to sleep?" Buzz stood there with a stunned look on his face.

"Who knows!" Jonathan began to panic. "It'll soon be totally dark. We need to look for the pieces of string."

They started walking as fast as possible, frantically shining their flashlights from side to side as they searched while frequently looking up for any sign of the mysterious object.

"Here's one," Buzz pointed out a piece of string tied to a low tree branch.

"There's another one," Jonathan said.

When they reached the narrow pathway beside the river, the forest was dark. They began to run.

"We have to get out of here, fast! It's just too scary with all the shadows," Jonathan said breathlessly.

As they approached the lake, an owl in one of the treetops gave a loud and eerie sounding "Hoo-oo-hoo" which echoed across the space over the lake. Then, with a rustle of feathers, it spread it's wings and flew silently over their heads and into the night.

"Hurry! Run!" Buzz said in a panic.

They ran to the edge of the forest where they got on their bikes and raced home as fast as they could.

When he arrived, Jonathan went inside his house and looked at the kitchen clock. It said 8 o'clock. He sat down at the table. *How could that possibly be? Nothing is making any sense. If that clock is right, about six hours just disappeared. I'm sure we didn't fall asleep and we didn't even eat the sandwiches we took for lunch.*

Suddenly, Jonathan felt very hungry. He hadn't eaten anything since breakfast. He quickly gobbled up his sandwich and chased it down with the juice. Then he went into the living room to try and figure out what happened while he waited for his mother to come home.

A short time later he heard her car pull into the driveway. She came into the house looking very tired.

"What did you and Buzz do today?" She sat down beside him on the sofa and put her feet up on the footstool.

"We just hung out." He couldn't possibly tell her where they had gone. She'd freak out. Suddenly, Jonathan realized how completely exhausted he was. "I think I'll go up to my room and listen to that CD I bought last week," he said. "I really like it."

# CHAPTER 3

## WAS IT A GHOST?

The next day right after breakfast Buzz arrived. Jonathan went outside and both boys sat down on the front steps, which was where they did their best thinking.

"What happened when you got home so late yesterday?" Jonathan asked.

"My mom had gone out to a restaurant with her friend," Buzz said. "She left my dinner on a plate with a note to nuke it. Dad had gone out of town to get some car parts for his repair shop and wasn't back yet. I sure lucked out."

"You're not kidding. My mom worked late so I was already home when she got here. I just can't figure out what happened to us, losing all that time and everything. It's way too weird. I think we need to go back to the cave and see if we can find out what's going on."

"What if we, like, passed out in there?" Buzz asked. "That could have happened, couldn't it?"

"I guess so," Jonathan slowly nodded his head. "But why would we do that?"

"Remember how we thought we heard something funny, like the swishing sound that big thing made?" Buzz asked.

"Yes. Maybe it did come back and gave off something in the air that knocked us out." Jonathan's imagination was going wild. "Let's go back now and see if we can figure this out. We're probably imagining things. Maybe the cave makes you do that."

"Who knows?" Buzz said. "It's like another world in there."

"I'll get fresh batteries and meet you in a few minutes." Jonathan went back inside the house.

Buzz jumped on his bike and went home.

Soon they met at the forest and began to search for the pieces of string tied to the bushes.

After passing by the first few markers, the pathway began to look familiar. When they reached the opening to the cave, Jonathan took the flashlight out of his pocket.

"I'm going in first," he said. "Take my watch. I brought it along so we can see if it does something funny inside the cave." He handed it to Buzz. "Give me about ten minutes, then call my name to make sure I didn't pass out or anything." Then he lay down on his stomach and slid through the opening."

Buzz just stood there with his mouth hanging open. Obviously, he had no idea what on earth he would do if that happened.

Jonathan followed the beam of the flashlight while he climbed down to the cave floor and went around the corner as they had done before. He entered the big grotto and sat down on the flat formation to wait.

When Jonathan heard his name ten minutes later, he stood up and returned to the entrance. "I'm still awake. I'm okay. Come on down."

Buzz twisted and squeezed his body through the opening, then climbed down. "I wonder if we'll ever find out what happened to us yesterday." he said.

"I don't know. I don't hear that strange noise we thought we heard. Do you?" Jonathan stood very still to listen.

"No, I don't think so."

"Let's go on through here. It's like a big room."

They stared around at the odd shapes coming down from the ceiling and the pillar-like formations on the walls as they passed through. At the far side, the wall seemed to split into two openings.

"Let's take the one on the right," Jonathan said. He led the way, shining the light all around as he proceeded to walk through it with Buzz behind him. The walls seemed to get closer the deeper they went into the passageway, until their shoulders were touching on either side.

"This is getting way too narrow. I wonder where it goes," Jonathan said. As he spoke, a sudden rush of air blew toward them, creating a high-pitched whistle.

"What was that?" Buzz stood frozen in place.

"It's just the wind," Jonathan tried to sound as reassuring as possible. "Maybe there's a small opening somewhere and that's why it sounded like that." He shone the flashlight up ahead where it illuminated two rocks with an opening between wide enough to squeeze through. At that moment, another gust of wind forced its way through, but this time it sounded more like a high-pitched scream. Then, out of the corner of his eye, Jonathan saw the flutter of what looked like a sheer, filmy substance floating beside him. At the same time he felt a hand rest gently on the top of his head.

"Buzz, d-did you j-just touch me?" he stammered.

"No, I didn't," Buzz answered. "What are you talking about?"

"Something just put its hand on top of my head. Let's get out of here!"

Because the opening was so narrow, they had to back out, Buzz first, then Jonathan. Then they turned around and, being careful where they stepped on the uneven floor, ran through the grotto until they reached the entrance.

"W-w-was that a ghost screaming?" Buzz asked as he quickly climbed up on the stones.

"I don't know." Jonathan felt a cold shiver running through his body as he followed Buzz. "But, I do know that was a hand I felt on the top of my head. And I saw something that you could see through, like material, sort of floating on the air."

"What! How could that be? I didn't see anything. Maybe I was looking down at where to put my feet. I think there was nobody there but you and me."

"I know, but it felt just like this." Jonathan put his whole hand on the top of Buzz's head. "Something or someone did that to me."

"Maybe it was a ghost, like the one we heard screaming."

"I don't think ghosts scream." Jonathan tried to calm both himself and Buzz. "They usually moan. I've only heard about them moaning."

"Yeah, I think you're right."

"It had to be just the wind. And maybe it blew my hair so hard it felt like a hand." Jonathan tried hard to convince himself. "What if that filmy thing was a spider web being blown around. They do live in caves."

"Yeah, that's probably it. And the noise we heard would be the wind. I don't think a ghost would scream for help anyway," said Buzz. "They only like to creep you out. Do you want to go back in there and see if it does it again?"

"No way! Not right now, anyway." Jonathan didn't want to admit he was still shaking inside.

They crawled out of the cave and headed for the lake.

"Here's your watch back," Buzz checked the time, then handed it to Jonathan. "See, it didn't do anything weird. We were in there for only a little while, less than an hour."

As they hurried along, they tried to make sense of the whole thing.

"That screaming could have just been a big bird screeching, like that owl or something," Buzz said hopefully.

"Yeah, maybe."

"If that huge shadow at the lake was made by a bird, and it made a lot of noise, it might have sounded like a scream," Buzz said.

Jonathan slowly nodded his head. "I guess it could."

When they got to the lake, they sat down on the grass by the edge of the water. A flock of Canada geese flew overhead and came in for a landing on the lake. They swam around bobbing for any plants in the water they could find to eat.

"Let's come back tomorrow and go to that same place," Jonathan said. "We need to have another look at it. Nothing bad ever happens. It's just totally weird."

"Yeah, I think we have to go," Buzz said. "Say, are you getting hungry? I'm starving."

"We didn't bring any food this time," Jonathan said. "Tomorrow, when we come back, we'd better take sandwiches. Do you want to go to my place? Mom made some tuna salad."

"Yeah, that's cool."

As they got up, their sudden movement disturbed the geese. They rose up together and flew away.

The boys headed for their bikes and took off. They rode along Jonathan's street and stopped in front of Mr. Grayson's house. Jonathan's elderly next-door neighbor was sitting on his porch, rocking back and forth with his eyes closed.

"Hi, Mr. Grayson," Jonathan called out as he and Buzz rode up the driveway.

"Hello, boys," Mr. Grayson opened his eyes and sat up straight. "How are you both doing today, and what are you up to?"

"We're fine, thank you," said Jonathan. "We just came from the forest."

"No kidding!" Mr. Grayson grinned. "See any dead bodies?"

"No, we were just looking around to see what's there," said Buzz.

"I tell you, that's one scary place," Mr. Grayson slowly shook his head. "You two are very brave going there all alone."

"It seems to be quite safe, really," Jonathan assured him.

"We think we may have found something to explore," said Buzz, mysteriously.

"Really? That sounds very exciting." Mr. Grayson's eyes lit up. "I never did go very far into the forest. After seeing that spirit I told you about a while ago, or whatever that was rising from the lake, I never went back."

"If what you saw was really a spirit," Buzz said, "I wonder if there might be more of them in the forest."

"You just never know." Mr. Grayson rocked back and forth a few more times.

Jonathan did not want to mention what they had just experienced. He needed to figure it out before telling anyone in case people thought they were crazy.

"Do you think a spirit could scream?" Buzz asked.

"I wouldn't be surprised," Mr. Grayson answered. "After all, they're tormented, which is why they can't just stay quiet and rest like they're supposed to. Be careful, boys."

"We will," Jonathan said as they hopped on their bikes. "We just came back for lunch."

Jonathan led the way inside his house and they headed straight for the kitchen. He put the loaf of bread and tuna salad on the table and they began to make their sandwiches.

"I think that with those openings and stuff that caves have, there must be wind blowing through there all the time," Buzz said. "We didn't hear any other noises, like animals or anything."

"You're right. There must be other ways to get in like the one we climbed through." Jonathan took a big bite out of his sandwich. "Let's go back early tomorrow."

"Yeah, we should. There's a lot more to that cave than we know about," said Buzz.

# CHAPTER 4

## A MAGICAL WORLD

Jonathan slept until the sun shining through his window woke him up. His mother had already left for work. He hurried downstairs and went straight to the phone to call Buzz. "Are we going back to the cave today?" He paused. "Okay. I'll meet you in half an hour. I guess we'd better bring something to eat this time."

After breakfast Jonathan made his usual lunch, put it in his backpack along the flashlight and set off. On their arrival, they hurried to the cave and climbed inside.

They went through the grotto and took the right pathway as before. When they passed through the ever-narrowing opening, Jonathan shone his flashlight all around to see if he could catch sight of the filmy vision, but there was no sign of it. They came to the two rocks with the space between, just wide enough to squeeze through sideways. As they proceeded it gradually opened up. What they saw was so unreal it made them stop, unable to speak. It looked as if they had entered another world. They stood in a narrow room with a waterfall cascading from the high ceiling. It splashed on crystalline ledges that shimmered in a hazy, bluish light. The light seemed to come from an opening up high that formed a skylight. Ferns emerged gracefully from openings in the walls, and moss covered some of the rock formations in the same area. On top of one of the rocks, three very large baby birds sat in a nest, their scrawny necks extended as they screeched loudly for their mother.

"Those birds sure look and act like babies," said Jonathan. "But how come they're so big?"

"I bet they'll be humongous when they grow up." Buzz couldn't stop staring.

Just then their mother, that looked like a bluejay but was the size of a large hawk, returned to her nest and began to feed the babies. They shrieked excitedly while awaiting their turn to be fed the food she had brought.

Directly in front of the boys, at the base of the waterfall, was a reflective pool that absorbed the blue from the skylight above. It was surrounded by pink and white lacy flowers. The result was a beautiful underground wonderland.

Suddenly, a very faint swishing sound from overhead brought the boys back to reality.

"Listen," Jonathan whispered. "It's that sound again."

"Yes, it is," Buzz nodded. "I bet it's the big shadow."

In an instant, the air was filled with fairy-like beings, fluttering their transparent wings and weaving in and out among the leaves of the ferns and the flowers by the pool. Their wings reflected the blue haze.

"How can this be?" Jonathan whispered. "It's like being in a Disney movie."

Buzz was speechless as he looked all around him.

Suddenly, one of the fairies turned and stared intently at Jonathan. As it did so, its eyes became piercing black beads and its face turned ugly. It grinned showing sharp, yellow teeth. In an instant, it changed back to its original appearance and continued to flutter its wings.

"Did you see that?" whispered Jonathan to Buzz who was staring up at the top of the waterfall.

"See what?"

"The face on one of those things changed. It was horrific."

"Are you for real?" Buzz asked in a low voice.

"Yes," Jonathan insisted. "It's true."

"I wish I'd seen it," Buzz whispered. "That's really scary."

The swishing sound continued for a few more minutes while the boys stood frozen, afraid to move and draw any more attention to themselves. The fluttering wings of the fairies continued as they slowly wafted their way in front of the waterfall and among the flowers until, just as suddenly as they had arrived, they disappeared and the sound stopped.

The boys stood looking at each other with their eyes as big as saucers.

"This can't be real," Jonathan shook his head. "I wonder if we could be hallucinating down here."

"It sure isn't normal," Buzz said.

"It might be something that happens in this part of the cave. Like yesterday when I felt that hand, or whatever it was, on top of my head. Maybe it was another one of those flying things. But the one I just saw makes me think there could be something really bad going on."

"But, at least they didn't try to hurt us," Buzz said. "Except for that ugly one, they just ignored us."

"Now that they're gone, let's get out of here." Jonathan led the way to the entrance and both boys climbed out. As they approached the lake, Buzz stopped suddenly. "Let's have our lunch before we go. We can sit by the water and chill out while we eat."

"That's a good idea." Jonathan sat down on the grass, leaned against a tree and stretched out his legs. Buzz sat beside him. They slowly ate their sandwiches, washing them down with the juice.

"At least it's normal out here," Buzz gave a big sigh.

Both boys sat quietly, looking out over the lake. Jonathan was beginning to relax. They watched as every now and then a fish swam up to the surface of the water in an attempt to catch an insect or some other floating object that caught its attention.

"We might as well go home," Jonathan said. "I don't feel like going back into the cave again today. Do you want to come back tomorrow and we can check out that other opening on the left side."

"Sure, that's cool," Buzz said. "Last night, my mom said I have to get my hair cut. She said it's beginning to look like a big mop. And this morning, my dad said the shelves in his garage need to be straightened up and restocked and he'll pay me for it. So that'll work. I've got plenty to do."

They got on their bikes and went home.

# CHAPTER 5

## THE MYSTERY DEEPENS

That night, Jonathan went to bed early. He was exhausted from all the excitement of his adventure in the cave. He soon fell into a sound sleep and began to dream.

*In his dream, he woke up in a daze. He got dressed, went outside and rode his bike to the forest. Then he ran all the way to the cave and crawled inside. He could hear strange-sounding voices. They were like muffled whispers, such as what you might hear with cotton in your ears. He followed the sound. It led to another room like the grotto, but smaller. It was crowded with shadowy figures dressed in floating white gowns, light as thistledown. They appeared to be suspended, weightless, just above the ground. One of them spotted Jonathan and whispered to the others. They began to crowd around him, and their whispers became a constant hum. He could feel them getting closer until he was completely surrounded. As they continued to close in on him, he felt he was being smothered. He tried to call out, but no words came.*

Jonathan sat up covered in sweat. He was shaking. *Where am I? Am I at home in my own bed?* He got up and looked out the window to be sure. The moon was shining so brightly it lit up the back yard. He was relieved to see his mother's flowers blooming in the border around the birdbath. The moonlight made the water sparkle and it shimmered in the gentle breeze.

Jonathan put on his slippers and tiptoed downstairs so as not to awaken his mother. He was afraid that if he went back to sleep right away, the dream would continue. He went to the kitchen, poured a glass of milk, and ate two of his mother's homemade oatmeal cookies. Then he returned to bed.

When Jonathan woke up, his mother had already left for work. He went straight to the phone and called Buzz.

"Do you want to meet today in about an hour?" He listened for a moment. "That's cool. I'll see you then. We'd better bring something to eat again."

After breakfast, Jonathan made his lunch, put it in his backpack, along with the flashlight, and headed for the forest.

As they walked to the cave, Jonathan didn't want to tell Buzz about his nightmare in case it spooked him so badly he'd want to go right home. But he just couldn't keep it to himself any longer.

"I had the worst nightmare last night," he said. "I was in the cave and there were ghosts all around closing in on me and I was so scared. I woke up and had to get out of bed because the dream was so real."

"No kidding. I didn't think about it at all once I got home," Buzz said. "I just figured we'd go back today and look around some more. But then, you thought a ghost, or something, touched your head. You know, it probably was just the wind like you said."

"Yeah," Jonathan smiled. "I think that sometimes nightmares are just stuff made up. At least, I hope so."

They reached the cave, climbed inside and headed for the main grotto. This time, they took the opening on the left. The pathway twisted and turned and they had to climb down several ledges to keep going until they reached the lowest level.

Buzz suddenly stopped. "Do you still have some of that string in your backpack so we can find our way back?"

"No, I took it out. I figured we'd only need it to mark the bushes. We just have to concentrate on which way we're going and come back the same way."

"Okay, but if we get lost, we could die and rot in here."

"We'll make sure that doesn't happen, don't worry," Jonathan assured him.

They continued on. Finally, the area through which they were walking opened up into a narrower grotto with another very high ceiling. The stalactites gave it the appearance of a small, but grand, cathedral.

As Jonathan shone the flashlight around, catching the beads of moisture from the glistening spires, suddenly, a very loud purring sound came from a ledge high up near the ceiling. It echoed throughout the grotto.

"What's that?" asked Buzz in a whisper. "It sounds like a very big cat."

"What kind of cat would you find in a place like this?" Jonathan stood perfectly still, afraid to move.

Buzz gasped. "I hope not the kind that likes to gnaw on people."

Jonathan shone the flashlight upwards, and the beam caught two yellow eyes looking back at him. He froze. A large cat stood up on the ledge where it had been sitting. It was the size of a lion. Around its neck, a blue and yellow striped collar with a silver bell sparkled in the beam from the flashlight. Its fur was the color of a gray pastel tortoise-shell cat, with a white mark under its chin. It stretched and yawned, meowed, then sat down and continued to purr. In the background, a very faint swishing sound could be heard.

"Let's get out of here," Jonathan whispered. They both quietly backed out of sight of the animal, then fled.

"That cat looked like a huge house cat," Jonathan continued to whisper as he ran. "Why would it have a collar on like that, with a bell too?"

"It looked so calm, as if it was friendly and tame," said Buzz.

"What's up with that purring?" Jonathan asked. "It was like it wanted to be petted."

"Yeah. And that sure would be a good way to lose an arm."

"I think the shadow might have been overhead," Jonathan said in a low voice. "Didn't you hear that strange sound again?"

"I didn't notice it with all the purring."

They reached the end of the pathway, hurried through the grotto and climbed out of the cave.

"I don't get it," Jonathan shook his head. "That cat didn't even seem to want to go after us. I just don't know what's going on in there."

"Me neither," Buzz shook his head.

"It's as if the thing that makes the shadow has some control over what happens in the cave. Any time there's something weird happening, you hear that sound overhead."

Jonathan stopped walking. "I'm getting so freaked out. Let's do something that's really different. It's still pretty early. Want to go bike riding?"

"Yeah. Good call, before we go nuts," Buzz laughed.

"We haven't gone riding around for a long time. Let's go downtown."

They hurried to their bikes and took off on the road that ran beside the forest. It was a cool, sunny day, perfect for being outside, and they raced each other in spurts until they reached Main Street.

"We could go into the Chuckwagon Grill and get something to drink. I feel like having a milk shake," Jonathan said. "Mom gave me my allowance just before she left for work this morning."

"Dad paid me yesterday for helping out at the garage," Buzz said. "I'm rich!"

When they arrived they locked their bikes to the lamp post by the front door and went inside.

The four swivel seats at the counter were empty, so they both sat down and spun around, as they usually did.

Tony, the owner, came up to the counter. "Well, boys, what'll it be today?"

"I'll have a large milk shake, please," Jonathan said.

"I'll have the same thing, thank you," said Buzz.

They spun around a few more times as they watched Tony fill up their glasses then set them on the counter.

Jonathan put his straw in and sipped it slowly. "How are we going to figure that thing out? Maybe it really is an alien spaceship."

"Wow! That would be so cool!" Buzz grinned.

"Did you know that aliens can kidnap you?" Jonathan asked.

"Huh?" Buzz's eyes were like saucers.

"Yeah, it's true. I read that in a book somewhere."

"What if that's what happened to those hunters that disappeared?" Buzz still looked stunned.

"Who knows," Jonathan said. "Nobody ever saw them again."

"Do you remember when Stevie Richards said he was in the forest and saw some aliens climbing out of a flying saucer, or something?"

"Yeah, I sure do," Jonathan said.

"And remember how Bobby Blunt and some of those other kids really mocked him for saying it?"

Jonathan slowly nodded his head. "Yeah. And that's why we'd better not say anything to anybody."

"No kidding!" Buzz agreed.

After they finished the shakes, they dug into their pockets, counted out the money and put it on the counter. Then they went outside and unlocked their bicycles.

"On our way home, do you mind if we stop at the library?" Jonathan asked. "I need to find a good book. Mom told me I have to turn off the TV and do some reading before the end of summer. It won't take long."

"Sure, I don't have anything else to do right now."

When they arrived, Buzz went to look at a magazine about cars while Jonathan approached the librarian's desk.

"Hi, Mrs. Bell," he said.

"Oh, Jonathan, I was just thinking about you." She stood up and reached for a book on the cart beside her desk. "This was returned a short time ago and I was going to call you because I remember you like mysteries." She handed it to him to look over. "It's fairly new and very exciting. The story is about two boys around the same age as you and Buzz. It's so well written I couldn't put it down until I had finished it."

"That sounds real cool. Thanks a lot, Mrs. Bell." He checked the book out and they hurried to their bikes and took off down the main road.

"What'll we do now?" Buzz asked.

"We didn't eat our sandwiches yet." Jonathan said. "I'm still hungry."

"Maybe we can pull over and eat someplace." Buzz said.

"Hey, look at that old wreck of a house." Jonathan slowed down as he pointed to a dilapidated building a short distance from the roadway. "That place has been falling apart forever. Nobody lives there anymore."

"Let's go and check it out. We can eat up there." Buzz turned his bike and both boys headed up the lane. When they reached the house, they got off their bikes and began to walk around the place.

"I wonder if the doors are locked." Buzz said.

"I don't know. We can try them. Let's eat first."

They took out their lunches, sat down on the grass and wolfed them down.

"What's in that other building?" Jonathan stood up and pointed to a beat-up shed at the edge of the property. Just then, out of the corner of his eye, he saw a flash of movement at one of the windows in the house. "Did you see that?" he asked.

"No, what was it?" Buzz, who was trying to pull open the cellar door, turned his head to look. "What did you see?"

"I saw something at this window. It was moving."

Buzz came closer, and both boys shielded their eyes with their hands from the reflection of the light on the glass as they peered through the dirty window. Suddenly, a cat jumped up on the window sill. It was a pastel gray tortoise-shell with a white spot under its chin. Around its neck rested a blue and yellow striped collar with a silver bell. The cat opened its mouth, meowed loudly enough for them to hear, then jumped down out of sight.

"Am I going crazy?" Jonathan asked. "That looks just like the big cat in the cave, only it's a normal size."

"I don't get it," Buzz scratched his head. "It can't be the same one. That's impossible."

"I'm getting so spooked!" Jonathan frowned. "It's as if when you go into that cave you're in another dimension."

"You're right," Buzz said. "There are ghosts that touch you, and house cats and birds that become humongous. What's that all about?"

"Maybe something in the cave makes us imagine things, like a dream." Jonathan said.

"What if it's real magic?" Buzz sat down on a broken step by the door. Jonathan sat beside him.

The cat returned to the window sill and scratched at the glass. Both boys got up and tapped on the window.

"Hello, Kitty," Buzz said. The cat pawed at the glass again and meowed.

"This is way too creepy," Jonathan shook his head. "I need to get home and think." He looked at his watch. "It's getting kind of late. We'd better go."

"We should come back and see if we can open that cellar door, and then try to find out what's inside the shed." Buzz said excitedly. "What if that cat is really the same one and this house connects to the cave?"

"We definitely need to come back," Jonathan said.

# CHAPTER 6

## A SECRET TUNNEL

The next day, Jonathan awoke to pounding on the front door. He looked at the clock beside his bed. It was 9 AM.

*I can't believe I slept so late.* He jumped up and hurried downstairs to open the door.

Buzz stood there with a wide grin on his face. "I just thought I'd come over because I can hardly wait to go back to that old house."

"Come in. Did you have breakfast yet?" Jonathan needed to know because the idea of going out for an adventure on an empty stomach was completely out of the question.

"Not really," Buzz said. "I didn't want to take the time. But I did make my lunch."

"We need to eat something before we go. Would you like a bagel and cream cheese? Mom bought some yesterday."

"Sure, thanks. That sounds good."

They went into the kitchen. Jonathan poured two glasses of orange juice. He split two bagels, put them in the toaster oven, then he set a container of cream cheese and a jar of strawberry jam on the table. When the bagels were slightly browned, he put them on a plate and they sat down.

"If you put strawberry jam on top of the cream cheese, it's really good." Jonathan demonstrated.

Buzz took a big gulp of juice, then followed Jonathan's example. "I hope we'll be able to open that cellar door," he said, and he took a bite out of the bagel.

"I'm sure we can get in. The whole place is such a wreck," Jonathan said. "I'll take a screwdriver or something to pry it open."

"That'll work," Buzz nodded.

"If we get that door open, we'll have to be very careful to keep the cat from getting out," Jonathan warned. "If it escapes, we'll never be able to figure out what's going on."

They finished eating and cleared the table.

"Thanks a lot for breakfast, Jonny. It was really good."

After Jonathan made his lunch with the usual peanut butter and jelly sandwich, they took off for the old house.

When they arrived, they went around to the back and parked their bikes.

"Let's check out the shed first," Buzz said. "If there's a car inside, we'd better get out of here fast."

The shed stood surrounded by tall grass and weeds. The wood was old and weathered and in need of a coat of paint.

"We should try and see if we can open the door with the screwdriver." Jonathan dug into his backpack. "The wood looks as if it's all rotten. This should be a piece of cake." The screws turned easily and the hasp came right off. He opened the door and they both went inside. An old, red pickup truck, that just fit into the small building, sat on four flat tires.

"This shows that nobody's been here for a long time, that's for sure," Jonathan said. The door on the driver's side was open, so he climbed in.

Buzz opened the other door. "What a mess! The stuffing in the seat's all coming out."

Jonathan tried to honk the horn, but it made no sound.

"The battery's probably dead after sitting here for so long," Buzz said. He was about to climb in when he heard a squeak coming from under the dashboard. "What's that?"

"I'll get the flashlight from my backpack outside the door." When Jonathan came back, he shone the light where the sound had come from. There, in a nest made from the seat stuffing, three baby mice were climbing all over each other while squeaking and shivering.

"Look how small they are," Buzz said. "They look cold, or maybe they're scared."

"We'd better go so the mother can come back," Jonathan put the flashlight into his pocket.

They got out of the truck, leaving the driver's side door open just as they had found it, and closed the shed door behind them.

"Let's see if we can open that cellar door." Buzz hurried to the door and pulled as hard as he could. "It's too tight. I can't budge it." He looked up as the cat, that had been lying on the window sill sunning itself, got up and pawed at the glass. "Look, Jonny. I bet it's wondering what we're doing."

"It probably wants to get outside." Jonathan carefully inspected the door knob which was quite loose. He worked at it with the screwdriver until it opened.

Both boys looked inside, cautiously, in case the cat was ready to escape, but it was nowhere to be seen. They went down the rickety steps into the basement, closing the door behind them. It was so dark inside that Jonathan took out his flashlight and shone it around the dismal room. There were no windows.

In the far corner an open stairway lead to the upstairs with a door partly off its hinges. There on the top step sat the cat. It meowed and came down to meet them, its silver bell ringing with each step. It approached Jonathan and rubbed against his leg.

"Can you believe this?" He bent over to stroke its head. "Now, we're going to have to go back to that same place in the cave and see if that humongous cat is there, and if it looks exactly like this one."

The cat started walking toward the back of the basement where several large pieces of rotting plywood leaned against the wall. It squeezed in behind and disappeared.

"Where did it go?" Buzz followed the direction the cat had taken. He took hold of a piece of the old wood, being careful to avoid the splinters, and moved it aside. It exposed an area of the wall that had been smashed open. They climbed through the hole, took a few steps down and found themselves at the entrance to a dirt tunnel.

"Let's see where this goes." Jonathan could hardly contain his excitement. "This might be turning into an amazing mystery." He stepped into the tunnel with Buzz behind him and shone the light ahead. It reflected three pairs of beady, little eyes that immediately disappeared as tiny feet scurried off.

"Oh, man, more mice!" Jonathan said in disgust.

"That's probably what the cat eats," Buzz said.

Strung along the side of the dirt tunnel was an electrical wire. Here and there, a bare light bulb dangled from a socket. The boys continued on past where some of the wiring had sagged nearly to the ground.

"I wonder who dug this tunnel, and why," Jonathan said. "It looks like it goes in quite far."

"Digging it would've taken a lot of work," Buzz said.

As they progressed underground, the dirt walls became solid on the right side, with huge, evenly cut rocks. The ground under their feet had now become firm and it appeared that they had reached an outer portion of something similar to a cave. Then, without warning, Jonathan's light began to flicker.

"Did you bring your flashlight?" he asked.

"No, I didn't think we'd need it just to get into the house."

"We've got to get out of here fast," Jonathan gasped in horror. "The batteries are dying. We'll never get back without a light." He began to panic.

Both boys turned and ran as fast as they could. Suddenly, Jonathan tripped and fell down with a thump. "Oh, no! My foot caught on a root, or something." With the impact from the fall, the flashlight went completely dead.

"Can you get up?" Buzz asked. "Do you need help?"

"No, my knee hurts, but I'm okay. I'm up," Jonathan answered.

"How are we ever going to find our way out? I can't see anything." Buzz's voice was trembling.

"We can just follow the dirt wall." Jonathan slid his feet across the earth until he came to the side of the tunnel. He reached his hand out. "Here's that electrical wire with the light bulbs on it," he said excitedly. "We can follow that right to the house."

With the wire as a guide, the boys slowly made their way to the broken wall and into the basement. They could see just a thread of light at the bottom of the cellar door to lead them in the right direction. Carefully, they felt their way up the rickety stairs, opened the door and stepped outside into the sunlight, closing the door behind them. They were both still shaking.

"I've never been so scared in my whole life," gasped Jonathan. He sat down to examine a bleeding scrape on his knee. "I think I landed on a stone or something when I tripped."

"Imagine what could have happened if that wire wasn't there," Buzz said. "We would have had to feel our way through the whole tunnel."

"Yeah, and with mice running around our feet, too! That's so disgusting. Just thinking about it is really creeping me out."

"What if one of them ran up your leg?" Buzz laughed.

A cold chill ran down Jonathan's back and he shuddered.

"What's up with all the wiring and light bulbs anyway?" Buzz wondered.

"Beats me!" Jonathan shook his head. "It's like somebody went through there a lot. What would anybody want to do that for? Why not just take a flashlight like we did?"

"I know, it just doesn't make any sense."

"Next time, we need to bring spare batteries, and we both need to bring a flashlight. We can't ever let that happen again," Jonathan said. "Let's go home."

# CHAPTER 7

## A Gruesome Surprise

The next morning, Jonathan looked in all the kitchen drawers for batteries for his flashlight. His mother kept a supply for when she worked the night shift. He found the box, but there were only two left. He knew he could not take the last two in case she needed them that night. He went upstairs to his bedroom and took his allowance from the desk drawer. Then he got his bicycle from the garage and set off for the grocery store.

On his way downtown, he passed Mrs. Smithfield's house. She was sitting on her porch drinking coffee and reading the newspaper.

"Good morning, Jonathan," she called out and waved. "Come here for a minute."

Jonathan pulled up into her driveway and stopped at the porch. In a small place like Jacobsville, most people knew everybody in town and those, like Mrs. Smithfield, knew everyone else's business.

"I hear you and Buzz Cameron have been going into the forest." she said.

"How did you hear that?" asked Jonathan. He didn't think anyone knew what he and Buzz were doing. Even his mother and Buzz's parents had no idea they had discovered a cave. In fact, nobody else he knew was even aware that a cave existed in that part of the forest.

"I was speaking to Maude Grayson and she said you and Buzz stopped by to talk to her husband."

"Yes, we did." Jonathan said. He wasn't sure where this conversation was going. "We went by the lake to hang out." Jonathan was very relieved when he realized that she knew nothing about their adventure.

"Mr. Grayson had a terrible fright at that lake years ago." She shook her head. "Maude said he never went back again. Apparently, he saw a spirit come out of the lake, and I think it went after him. It scared him half to death. Are you boys safe in that place?" She looked quite worried.

"Yes we are," Jonathan assured her. "Mr. Grayson told us all about what happened to him. The spirit didn't chase him. It just stayed over the lake. We've found that the forest is quite safe or we wouldn't go there."

But Mrs. Smithfield persisted. "I've heard that hunters have been lost somewhere in the forest and were never seen again. Maybe they were eaten by wild animals." She shuddered. "I know there are wolves and coyotes in there. My friend, Agnes, lives right at the edge of the forest and she said she can hear them howling at night."

"The forest is huge," Jonathan said. "Maybe those hunters just went in too far. We always know where we're going." He backed his bike away from the porch. "I have to go on an errand to the store now, so I'll be seeing you." He took off in a hurry, glad to have an excuse to escape any more of her questions.

Jonathan rode downtown and bought the batteries. When he returned he went straight to Buzz's house. Buzz had just returned from his father's service station with his own batteries.

"My dad wondered what I needed them for," he said. "I told him we wanted to be able to see so we could dig for worms in the backyard at night. Then we'd be ready if we decided to go fishing at the lake first thing in the morning."

"Good thinking," Jonathan said. "I'm going home to make a lunch and get ready, and I'll meet you there in an hour. Okay?"

"Yeah, see you." Buzz went back inside.

After the boys met at the forest, they walked beside the lake, looking up as usual for the mysterious shadow. But, whatever it was, they hadn't seen it again.

They reached the cave and climbed inside.

"First, we need to see if that humongous animal is there," said Jonathan. "If it looks just like the cat in the house, I'll be totally freaked out."

"Yeah, me too. That's like something from a sci-fi movie."

As they had both brought flashlights, the inside of the cave was much better illuminated. They followed the lights through the grotto and took the left opening to retrace their steps. They proceeded through its twists and turns and carefully climbed down the ledges until they reached the lowest level. From there they entered the narrow grotto with the high ceiling. They flashed their lights around the stalactites, causing the reflections to bounce around forming eerie patterns. But there was no sign of the animal.

"If it's the same cat, then it must have some way of getting into the house," Jonathan said. "That opening in the wall ahead looks as if it's the only other way to get through here, so let's try it, okay?"

Buzz hesitated for a moment. "I guess we could." He tried hard to work up his courage.

The opening was a narrow extension of the grotto with the same high ceiling. They had just gone a short distance when they noticed a narrow side opening between two large stalagmites that led in another direction.

"I wonder where that leads to." Buzz said.

"We'd better just keep going on this pathway so we don't get lost." As Jonathan shone his flashlight toward the opening, it caught what looked like a pile of thin pieces of white wood leaning against one of the stalagmites. They went closer, then froze.

"Oh, man! Yecch!" Jonathan backed up. "It's a skeleton of some kind of animal. It looks like a dog, or a wolf or something."

"What's that in its mouth?" Buzz's lip curled up. "Eeeww! Gross! It must have been eating that thing when it died."

"Look," Jonathan, pointed to the top part of the animal's skull. "It's smashed in. It looks like part of that column broke off and bonked it on the head." As both boys stood gazing down at the bones, a black image flew in a circle high over their heads. The flashlight created an eerie shadow on the ceiling much larger than the object itself. Then, several more black figures flew closer to the boys, criss-crossing as they went. They made high-pitched chirping sounds while swooping down low, then circled around. Both boys put their hands over their heads to shield them. The creatures came back, this time diving much lower as if trying to attack them.

"A-a-are those b-bats?" Buzz asked in a shaky voice. "I saw some on TV. They live in caves and they sound sort of like birds just the way these things do." He shone his light up to try and follow one in flight.

"I saw a picture of a bat once," Jonathan said as he ducked down. "It looked really scary, with horrible, spiky teeth."

"We need to get out of here," Buzz said. "I-I've heard people say that a bat can get in your hair. That would be so scary. What if you couldn't get it out and it just kept chirping and fluttering its wings on top of your head?"

Jonathan was so horrified by that thought, he quickly turned around to high-tail it out of the cave, but the bats were swooping down so low behind him, it was impossible to escape.

"There's no other way to get away from them but to go in farther." Still holding his hands on top of his head, Jonathan screamed, "Run!"

They took off as fast as possible along the narrow, winding pathway, being careful not to trip on the uneven surface. Eventually, they left the bats behind and were able to slow down and catch their breath.

"M-man, that was a c-close one," Buzz stammered.

"Yeah, you're not kidding. What if one of them bit us? They could have rabies or something." As Jonathan was speaking he aimed his flashlight up ahead. "Wouldn't it be cool if this pathway lead right to the house?"

"Yeah, and if the two cats are the same, that would explain how it got in and out of there," Buzz said in an excited voice.

"You know, Buzz, we might even be able to solve the mystery of all this crazy stuff."

Jonathan shone his light up high and it caught the reflection of what looked like a fine, metal chain that seemed to be hanging from one of the tall stalagmites. As he raised the light beam higher, he couldn't believe what he saw. Impaled on the spike at the top of the formation, was a partly decomposed body, its head and feet were draped on either side, with the chain dangling from around its neck.

"Look," Jonathan gasped, pointing a shaky finger. He couldn't stop trembling and he felt goose bumps all over his body.

Buzz just stood there frozen. "I-I think I'm going to barf," was all he could manage to say.

Jonathan, who thought he could still hear the bats chirping behind him, felt his stomach beginning to churn. "Let's get out of here!" he shouted.

They took off as fast as they could. After a short distance they began to notice that the ground under their feet was no longer hard as in the cave, but soft, like earth. The flashlight picked up a row of sagging wire, with light bulbs attached, running along the wall.

"We're in the tunnel behind the house," Jonathan shouted. "There's that same wire."

"Yeah, b-but whose body is that?" Buzz asked, obviously still shaken up. "What's he doing stuck on that thing?"

"Maybe he fell from someplace higher up." Jonathan said. "We're going to have to call the police."

# CHAPTER 8

## THE STORM

Jonathan and Buzz each shone their flashlights ahead as they hurried through the tunnel to the deserted house. When they reached the hole into the basement, they slid the rotting plywood to the side and crawled through. There was no sign of the cat as they opened the cellar door, stepped outside and closed it behind them.

The sky was very dark, as thick, black storm clouds rolled in.

"It looks as if it's going to rain soon," Buzz said. "We'd better get home."

"Oh, no," Jonathan sighed. "I forgot that we parked our bikes where we went into the forest."

"Oh, rats!" Buzz said. "That's probably a mile or more away."

"Well then, we need to start running right now or we'll get soaked." They both took off down the driveway and turned onto the shoulder of the main road. They raced toward the forest entrance as the sound of thunder rumbled in the distance.

"I hope we'll make it home in time," Buzz panted.

Just then, a flash of lightening streaked across the sky. It was followed by a louder clap of thunder. The boys ran even faster.

"I remember reading that when the thunder and lightening come close together, the storm is nearly overhead." Jonathan gasped."

Almost ready to collapse, they finally reached the forest entrance. They retrieved their bicycles from behind the bushes and took off for home pedaling as fast as they could.

They had just reached Jonathan's house when a powerful flash of lightening lit up the whole sky. It was followed immediately by a deafening clap of thunder. They quickly put their bicycles in the garage and closed the door, just as a torrent of rain began to pour down.

They proceeded through the garage and into the kitchen.

"I'd better call my mom so she'll know we're okay," Jonathan said and he picked up the kitchen phone. After speaking with his mother, he handed the phone to Buzz. "Tell your mom you can hang out here as long as you need to, okay? My mom said she may have to stay at work later because the streets are flooding."

After Buzz finished his call and hung up, they headed for the living room. The room was getting so dark, Jonathan turned on the lights.

"Let's get the weather channel on TV and see what's happening." Jonathan turned the set on and they both sat down. "We'll go to the police when it clears up. They can't do anything now, anyway. They'll be pretty busy."

"Yeah, that poor guy isn't going anywhere." Buzz got up to look out the window just as a bolt of lightening zigzagged straight down from the sky. It hit the transformer on the telephone pole at the end of the block with a loud *bang*. This was followed immediately by a thunder clap so loud it made both boys jump. The TV began to sputter, then died as the power went off, plunging the room into darkness.

"Wow! That sounded too close," Jonathan said. "At least we made it into the house in time."

Suddenly a powerful gust of wind snapped off a branch from the tree in the front yard and blew it against the living room window.

Jonathan jumped up to look. "It's like a tornado or something." A dusty-looking funnel could be seen in the sky about a mile away, moving along the edge of town at a fast rate, picking up branches and other debris and swirling them around while the wind howled.

Both boys watched as the tree in the front yard, now violently swaying back and forth, was lifted up by its roots. With a loud thump, it landed flat on the ground. As they stood there with their hearts pounding, they heard a crash that seemed to come from next door. They looked on in horror, as Mr. Grayson's rocking chair, that had apparently been lifted from his porch, took off bouncing down the street, breaking into pieces as it went.

"Oh, no," Jonathan gasped. "This is getting really bad. You don't know what'll happen next. I'm going to call Mom and tell her what's going on." He picked up the phone, but the line was dead.

The wind continued to blow, but its energy seemed to be weakening. Soon a deadly quiet fell on the town. The sky had a yellow tint to it as the storm clouds gradually moved away. Both boys continued to stare out the window. The street was flooded, but a truck managed to come through, creating small waves as it passed by.

"This street is higher than the next block, so the water should run off soon," Jonathan said. "It always does that if it rains hard."

"I think the storm's over," Buzz sighed. "I hope it doesn't come back. What do we do now?"

"I guess we just wait," Jonathan said. "It's already after two o'clock and we didn't eat yet. I'm starving. Did you bring a sandwich with you?"

"Yes, I did," said Buzz, and he got the backpack that he had set on the kitchen floor.

They took their lunches to the living room and ate while sitting and waiting by the window.

A short time later, two trucks from the power company slowly approached. One stopped at the pole in front of the house, and the other proceeded to the transformer. The boys stood watching the cherry picker on the truck lift one of the workers up high beside the pole.

After a few minutes, the lights went on. Jonathan hurried to the TV. "Let's see if there's anything about the storm on the weather channel."

A newscaster was just beginning his report:

*An unusual tornado has hit Jacobsville, Wisconsin, a small town at the eastern edge of the Great National Forest. The affect has been devastating. The surveillance helicopter reported that a wide swath of trees in that part of the forest have been downed. This is the worst storm to hit the town in over 100 years. We will keep you posted as more information becomes available.*

"I'd like to see that part of the forest that was hit," Jonathan said. "I hope it isn't near where we go."

"Yeah. What if we can't get back to the cave?" asked Buzz.

"We can always go to the old house to get in," Jonathan said. "I hope the place wasn't damaged and the cat's okay."

"It probably hid somewhere. Cats are good at hiding."

Just then the telephone truck pulled up in front of the house. Soon the job was finished and the service was restored.

"I need to call my mom to tell her what happened," Jonathan headed for the phone. "Mom, the storm was terrible here. The tree at the front where my swing used to hang was blown over. Even the roots were pulled up. Wait 'til you see the mess." He listened for a moment. "Okay, Mom, see you later." He handed the phone to Buzz so he could call home.

"We're okay," Buzz assured his mother as he told her what had happened. Then he turned to Jonathan. "Dad's coming in the truck to pick me up with my bike."

"Okay. As soon as the water drains off the road, we'll be able to ride to the police station and report the body," Jonathan said.

# CHAPTER 9

## THE AFTERMATH

That evening, Jonathan's mother arrived home from work late. When she came in the door, she headed straight for the living room and collapsed on the sofa. Jonathan followed her into the room and sat down.

"I've never seen such a disaster in my whole life." She put her feet up on the footstool. "It took me over an hour to get home instead of my usual 15 minutes."

"No way! How did you get here?"

"I tried several roads, but they were all blocked by fallen trees." She gave a long sigh. "Finally, I got through one of those narrow back streets, but I had to weave around several garbage cans that had emptied all over the road. Wouldn't you know, tomorrow is pick-up day so everybody's garbage was out."

"Wow, what a mess that must have been," Jonathan said. "Buzz and I were really scared when the wind got so strong it started blowing everything around at the front of the house."

"Yes, I'm sure you were. I noticed the damage when I pulled up. I'll have to call someone to remove that tree. At least I was able to get into the garage."

She sat quietly for a moment, then put her head back against the sofa. "Downtown, those beautiful planters in front of the stores were blown over onto the road and smashed. And siding and roof tiles that were ripped off some of the buildings are scattered on the ground. There was no way I could get through. I could see Tony down the street, standing outside of the Grill and just staring." She sighed again. "I'm sure he's in shock, poor man."

"Buzz and I were there just yesterday," Jonathan said.

"Dear, I think you had better stay home tomorrow. It's way too dangerous for you and Buzz to go any place."

"Okay, Mom," he said.

"Why don't you read your library book? You said you thought it looked really good. Those trucks will be all over town clearing the roads of debris," she said. "It's going to take some time to get everything back to normal."

Jonathan was glad to have an excuse to not go to the police yet. He wasn't sure about how he could explain to them why he and Buzz had broken into the old house in the first place, even though it had been empty for a long time and was practically falling down. He certainly wasn't ready yet to tell his mother about exploring the cave and finding the body. In fact, he knew she wouldn't have approved of any of it. It wasn't as if he had planned on all those things happening. They just did.

The next day, Jonathan spent the morning reading, with occasional TV breaks to check the local news. The tornado had made such a huge impact on Jacobsville that reporters from the Woodland Chronicle were kept busy with video cameras recording the destruction and cleanup. Several trucks passed by his house pulling wood chippers, and he could hear the chain saws cutting the fallen trees at the end of the street. By this time, most of the water on the road had drained away.

Later that afternoon, Buzz called to say his father would drop him off for about half an hour, if it was okay. He had to take the tow truck to bring a disabled car to his garage, and would pick him up on the way back.

"Yeah, it sure is okay," Jonathan said. "It's getting kind of boring here. The trucks are finished working on this street, so there's nothing going on."

Soon Buzz appeared at the door. "Mom told Dad to drop me off here because I was driving her crazy. I couldn't stop eating. I do that when I'm bored."

"I'm glad she did," Jonathan said. "Come and sit in the living room. We need to talk about what we should do when we report that dead guy to the police. We can't say anything in front of our parents. My mom might go ballistic."

"Yeah, my mom, too," Buzz said.

"First of all, we don't want to have to tell them that we were exploring the cave. They would think that was way too dangerous," Jonathan said.

"Yeah, but what about the police?" Buzz asked. "If we had no choice but to confess that our parents didn't know about it, they would jump right on that and call them."

Jonathan stood thinking for a moment. "You know what, Buzz? I don't think we have to say anything at all about the cave. We could start with when we went to the old house and saw the cat inside and were worried about it."

"Cool idea!" Buzz said. "Then, we went in to make sure it was okay and it wasn't hungry or anything."

"We don't ever want to talk about any of those weird things we saw in the cave, you know, the fairies, or whatever they were. And the thing touching the top of my head, like I know it did," Jonathan said. "We wouldn't want the kids at school to hear about any of that stuff."

"Yeah, we'd never hear the end of it. We might even have to change schools," Buzz said.

"And the reporters from the Woodland Chronicle would want to interview us and take our pictures," Jonathan shook his head. "We'd have to find somewhere to hide for the rest of our lives."

"We still don't know what that big shadow was. I'd like to know. What if it was a spaceship?" Buzz asked.

"It might have been. Every time one of those weird things happened inside the cave, we heard that same swishing sound that it made when it floated over our heads in the forest." Jonathan said.

"Yeah. Then what about those dog bones, or whatever they were, and the bats dive-bombing at us," Buzz asked.

"I think those things are normal. They're not from outer space," Jonathan said. "Bats live in caves, and animals can get lost there, and starve to death, or get hurt and stuff."

Just then a loud *HONK* sounded from the front of the house.

"There's Dad," Buzz said, and he got up and started walking to the front door.

"You know, Buzz, before we do anything, we need to see if the house is still standing after the tornado, and if the entrance to the cave has been blocked off. The news on TV said a lot of trees in the forest were blown over."

"Maybe we won't be able to get in again," said Buzz. "Then we can definitely tell the police about just the house and the body. Nobody needs to know about the cave, ever."

"Yeah. Let's call each other tomorrow," Jonathan said. "We can't report anything until we've checked it all out."

# CHAPTER 10

## SAVED BY THE STORM

The next morning, Jonathan was awakened by the sound of a chain saw cutting up the fallen tree on his front lawn. He went to the living room window to watch as two workmen loaded the huge pieces of wood on a truck, and left. It was already after nine o'clock.

Jonathan went to the living room and turned on the television to see if there were any more reports about the tornado on the local channel. But a man on an infomercial was demonstrating how to build a deck on the back of a house, so he went to the kitchen, poured cereal into a bowl, added milk and hurried back to the TV. The local announcer had just come on:

*The cleanup in Jacobsville is continuing at a fast pace so the town can get back to its usual business. The main street has been cleared of debris, and this morning most of the stores are open.*

There was no further mention of the forest or surrounding areas. Jonathan finished eating and phoned Buzz. "We're going to check out the cave entrance first, right?" He listened for a moment. "Yeah, we'll definitely need flashlights for the cellar when we get to the house. I'll meet you in half an hour."

Quickly, Jonathan made his lunch and put it in his backpack. Then he hurried to the garage for his bicycle, met Buzz and they set off for the cave.

"Look at all the leaves and stuff floating on the water," Jonathan said as they passed by the lake. "That storm made an awful mess." Three Canada geese were attempting to swim around, bobbing for food among the leaves and making waves as they ploughed through. Several small trees had been uprooted and were lying on the ground, along with numerous broken branches, which made walking very difficult.

"The reporter showed a photo of a wide swath of trees that had been uprooted," Jonathan said. "But he didn't say where the picture had been taken. Maybe it wasn't even here, but closer to the Minnesota border on the other side of the forest."

When the boys finally arrived at the cave, they stopped and stared in disbelief. A very large tree had been uprooted by the storm and crashed directly in front of, and up against the entrance. The trunk was so wide, you could not tell if any of the rocks had been dislodged.

"Do you suppose anybody ever saws up fallen trees in the forest?" Jonathan wondered. "They might just let them rot and go back to nature. We'll have to wait and see what happens. Right now, this looks pretty hopeless."

"Yeah, it sure does." Buzz sounded very dejected.

They turned around and walked slowly back. As they approached the lake, a frog hopped quickly across their path and disappeared into the water.

"We might as well eat right here," Jonathan suggested. "We may be too busy later." They sat down on a log and slowly ate their lunch while looking out at the lake.

When they had finished, Buzz began to perk up.

"We have to see if that cat's still alive. I hope the tornado missed the house."

"Yeah, I hope so too." Jonathan jumped up. "Let's go right now!"

They hurried to their bikes and took off down the road. On reaching the house, they rode up the driveway. In the past, the property had been partly hidden by several evergreen trees, but today the house seemed to be more exposed as some of the trees had apparently just disappeared.

"Where's the shed?" Jonathan couldn't believe his eyes. The red pickup truck had apparently been lifted up by the strong wind, spun around, and was now facing the house. The hood was up and nearly twisted off.

"Look over there!" Buzz pointed to the far edge of the property. "It's like the shed's been all smashed up and blown all over the place."

"We'd better see if the baby mice are still alive." They hurried over to the truck. Carefully, both boys peered inside the cab and aimed their flashlights under the dashboard. Tucked deep inside, the tiny mice were still huddled in their nest.

"They look fine," Buzz smiled with relief.

"I think the mother must have found them. Let's get back to the house." Jonathan was beginning to worry. "We need to see if the cat's okay."

They hurried up the steps to the back porch and tapped on the window. At first, there was no response. Then they knocked loudly, and the cat came bounding up onto the sill.

"Hello, Kitty," they both said, as they lightly tapped the windowpane. The cat reached its paw up as if to touch them.

"Thank goodness it wasn't hurt," said Jonathan. "Let's see if we can get inside." They went to the cellar door and tried to force it open. After two tries, they were able to get in. They closed the door behind them and turned on their flashlights. The cat immediately appeared and began to purr, rubbing against first Jonathan's leg, then Buzz's.

"I think it's really glad to see us," said Buzz.

Jonathan bent over and stroked it gently. "It must have been so scared. At least there's plenty of food to eat with all the mice running around in here." He picked the cat up and held it in his arms. It purred loudly. "Sure is friendly." He put it back down, gently.

"Let's make sure we can get into the tunnel," Buzz said. "We have to be able to find the body so we won't look stupid when we go to the police."

"Yeah," Jonathan agreed. "You need to sound as if you know what you're talking about when you report something to them. We don't want them to just stand there rolling their eyes at us."

The boys shone their flashlights toward the back of the basement and followed the beams to the piece of plywood covering the tunnel opening. They pulled it aside and crawled through.

"It smells kind of damp in here, doesn't it?' asked Jonathan.

"Yeah, I guess it's because of that rain," Buzz said.

"Probably the water seeped in because this house is so old," Jonathan said. "It must have a lot of leaks."

They continued through the tunnel, with its wires and dark, scary spaces, until the earth underfoot became more solid.

"We're in the cave now," said Buzz.

"Yeah, you're right. And I think if we just keep going in this direction, we'll find the body." Jonathan kept shining the light up and to the left to see if it would catch the reflection of the chain dangling from around the man's neck. "I wonder where he was when he fell down onto that spike. Why was he up there anyway, and what was he doing?"

"I don't know," Buzz said, "but it would make a real good mystery if we could find out. Before we report this, let's see if we can figure out how he got up there."

"Yeah, that's a good idea."

Just then, Jonathan's light caught the reflection of the chain and both boys stopped to look up at the body. "He's still there, just as he was before. Let's go back and see if there's some sort of opening off this pathway that would take us behind where he is."

They retraced their steps and sure enough, a narrow opening between two stalagmite pillars allowed them to squeeze through. Just behind where the body hung, a ladder leaned against one of the pillars. At the top of the ladder a shelf had formed between two columns, joining them. Jonathan could see the corner of a chest-like box on top.

"I'm going to climb up and see what that is," he said.

"You can't do that!" Buzz shook his head. "Look what happened to him when he did it. You could die too."

"I'll be careful," Jonathan said, and he put his flashlight in his pocket to free both hands. "I'll just go up one rung at a time, slowly. Keep your light shining on me." He reached out to push on both columns, to see how strong they were. They were quite wide at the bottom, and seemed sturdy enough, so he climbed up the first rung. "It's good." Then he climbed up the second rung, then the third. "It's still okay," he said.

Buzz held onto the bottom of the ladder as tightly as he could while watching Jonathan take the fourth rung, then the fifth, and finally he stopped.

"I can see the box and touch it." He climbed another rung and reached up to open the box. "There are hard stones, or something in here." He climbed up one more rung, took the flashlight out of his pocket and shone it inside. "These things must be jewelry. They're all sparkly and look like necklaces. And I can see rings, too." Then he looked over to where the body was impaled and realized he was looking down at it. "Eewww." He began to shake. "I'm looking right at the dead guy's face. It looks really gross."

"Come down, right now," Buzz said. "I'm freaking out here."

"Hang on, I'm coming," Jonathan said. "I'm bringing a necklace as evidence." He closed the lid of the box and put the necklace in his pocket.

Slowly, he climbed down, one rung at a time, until he reached the bottom. He was starting to sweat from nervousness. "I can't stop shaking," he said when he finally placed both feet on solid ground. "Let's get out of here."

They both squeezed back out between the two columns and headed toward the tunnel and the old house. Once inside the basement, they opened the door, stepped outside and closed the door behind them.

"Now, we can go to the police," Jonathan said.

# CHAPTER 11

## REPORT TO THE POLICE

"Sergeant Graham," Jonathan said as he read the name plate on the counter at the Jacobsville Police Department. "We would like to report a dead body."

Sergeant Bruce Graham stopped typing on his computer, turned his head to face the boys, and with a puzzled look on his face said, "A what?"

"A dead body," repeated Jonathan.

The officer stood up and stepped to the counter. "Now, boys, what's this all about?"

"We were at that old deserted house with the long driveway by the forest," Jonathan said.

"Nobody lives there anymore, and it's real old and half falling down," Buzz added.

"I know the one you mean," said the officer. "What were you two doing there?"

"We were bike riding and we thought we'd go up and see the house," Jonathan said. "It looks as if nobody owns it."

"Well, somebody does own it, I'm sure," Officer Graham said. "But, what's this about a dead body?"

Jonathan continued. "We went around to the back and saw a cat sitting at the window inside."

"It was a gray, pastel tortoise-shell with a white mark under its chin," Buzz said.

"And a blue and yellow striped collar with a silver bell," Jonathan added.

"Well, that's odd," said the officer. "Sounds like someone's pet. I wonder if it's trapped in there. It could be starving to death."

"Oh, no," Jonathan said. "There are plenty of mice inside for it to eat."

"How do you know that?" asked the officer.

There was a long pause as Jonathan swallowed hard. "We went inside to see if it was okay."

"How did you get in?"

There was another long pause. *Oh, no.* Jonathan thought. *Now we're really going to be in trouble.*

"We pried open the cellar door with a screwdriver," said Buzz.

"Well, boys, we have an interesting expression for that sort of thing. It's called breaking and entering."

The color drained out of Jonathan's face and Buzz's eyes nearly popped right out of his head.

"B-b-breaking and entering?" they stammered together.

"We just had to know if the cat was okay," Buzz insisted.

"All right," the officer said. "But, how on earth did a dead body get involved in this?"

"Well, when we went inside we were in the basement and the cat came down from upstairs," Jonathan explained. "It was real friendly."

"It was purring and rubbing against our legs, and everything," said Buzz.

"Then it went to the back wall of the basement and disappeared through a hole," Jonathan said.

"Yeah." Buzz was getting so nervous his hands were beginning to shake. "We followed it through the hole, and ended up in a tunnel with old l-lires and w-wights, I mean wires and lights strung up on the walls." In his excitement, the words came out all jumbled up.

"Now, boys," the sergeant smiled, "stay calm. What you have just described is very interesting indeed. Go on."

"We went through the tunnel and ended up in a cave." Jonathan hadn't really wanted to mention the word *cave*, knowing that their secret adventures might get them some serious grounding by their parents. But he had no choice. He watched the officer's face when he said it.

"Wait a minute. You mean that house is connected to the cave in the forest by a tunnel?"

"Yes, it is."

"But, where's the body?" he asked.

"It's stuck on top of a spiky stalagmite," said Jonathan.

"A what?"

"A stalagmite. You know, those things in caves that stick up from the ground and the stalactites that come down from the ceiling," explained Jonathan, feeling very knowledgeable.

"Oh, yes, I know what you mean. I'm just not much on going into caves," said the sergeant. "I am aware of the cave in the forest. I didn't know it could be connected to a private home."

"Well, that's where the body is," Jonathan said. "He must have slipped and fallen on one of the spikes."

"And there's a ladder in back of him, higher up," said Buzz.

"Hold on a minute," said the officer. "I'd better get Chief Lomax involved here. This sounds very serious." He went to the door of the chief's private office, knocked and entered. After a brief conversation, he returned and ushered the boys into the office.

"Boys, this is Chief Andrew Lomax." He then left and closed the door.

Both boys stood at attention, waiting to be told what to do.

"Hello, boys," Chief Lomax said. "Please have a seat."

They slowly sat down on the two polished mahogany arm chairs, and folded their hands in their laps.

"Now, what are your names?" the chief asked.

"I'm Jonathan Taylor, Sir."

"I'm Buzz Cameron, Sir."

"Relax, boys." The chief smiled. "Sergeant Graham tells me you have discovered a body in the cave in the forest."

"Yes, Sir," Jonathan managed to say, with a crack in his voice.

"Would you please go over again how you came across this body?"

Jonathan began. He repeated the same story he had told the desk sergeant, with Buzz adding details here and there.

Chief Lomax looked over his glasses as he said, "Now, you know you had no business breaking into that house, no matter how rundown it is. For one thing, a place like that could be very dangerous. Wood in such bad condition can collapse right under your feet. And what you did is illegal. Do you understand that?"

"Yes, Sir, we do," Jonathan said, and both boys nodded in agreement, with their heads down, looking at the floor.

"It seems that you two have stumbled on a very interesting situation that needs to be looked into. Now, exactly where is the body?" He picked up his pen to begin taking notes on a pad of paper.

"It's on the other end of a dirt tunnel, with a row of lights on the side," Jonathan said. "But I don't think they'd be working anymore because they're sort of sagging down."

"When you get into the cave, you can see the body high up on the left side," Buzz said. "He's stuck on a spike."

"On a spike? How'd he manage to get up there in the first place? And I wonder how long he's been there," the chief looked puzzled.

"Probably quite a while," Jonathan said. "He doesn't look too good. I saw him face to face when I looked down on him."

"You what?" The chief's jaw dropped. "How did you get up there?"

"There's a place between two columns of stalagmites where you can squeeze through," said Jonathan. "And a ladder is leaning against one of the pillars. I guess he used it to climb up to his treasure chest."

"What's that you said? A treasure chest?" The chief raised his eyebrows as he sat up very straight in his chair.

"Yeah," Buzz said, and his voice rose. "Jonathan climbed up the ladder and found a ledge with the chest on it."

"It's filled with jewelry." Jonathan reached into his pocket and pulled out the necklace. "Here's one of the pieces I brought to show you."

Chief Lomax took the necklace in his hand and examined it carefully. "It looks real, but we'll have to have a jeweler look at it." He held it up and it sparkled in the sun shining through the window. "There were several robberies in Jacobsville about three years ago, and I remember one was at Robinson's jewelry store. That case was never solved."

The chief looked down at his desk calendar. "Today has been very quiet so far. Let me get in touch with my deputy, Dave Adam. He'll come with us and take some photographs and we'll be able to see and record the evidence for ourselves. With that box full of jewelry, this certainly does look like a crime scene, even though the man's death appears to be an accident. I will have to speak to your parents, because we will need you boys to show us exactly where the body is. I am very familiar with the cave, but with all the twists and turns, it might be difficult for us to find the exact spot on our own."

Jonathan knew this time would come. He and Buzz would have to tell their parents the whole story.

"Are your parents home now?" the chief asked.

"My mom's at work at the hospital," said Jonathan.

"What is her name?" asked the chief.

"Jean Taylor. She's a nurse there."

"Buzz, is your mother home?"

"I don't think so," Buzz answered. "But my dad is at work at Cameron's service station. He owns it."

"Okay, boys. Why don't you have a seat in the waiting room while I call and get their permission, then we'll go." The chief picked up the phone.

Jonathan and Buzz left the room and sat down across from Sergeant Graham.

"I wonder what my mom will say when she gets the call," Jonathan said. "She always worries so much."

"Yeah, my parents too," Buzz said. "I bet they didn't know that the cave was even there."

A few minutes later, Chief Lomax came out of his office. "We're all set, boys. Dave, my deputy, will meet us over there. Both your parents seemed quite shocked that you found a body. I'm sure they will have lots of questions to ask you when you get home."

Jonathan and Buzz looked at each other with worried expressions on their faces. They got into the police car and sat in the back seat in complete silence while the chief drove them to the old house.

When they arrived, Dave was leaning against his car waiting, with a camera bag slung over his shoulder. He approached the squad car as the boys were getting out. "Hi there," he said. "I hear you boys have been drumming up some business for us in the cave. You sound like a couple of pretty good detectives."

Both boys smiled at that, but said nothing.

"What's that mess of wood over there, and the old pick-up truck?" asked the chief.

"The tornado must have come through here," explained Jonathan. "The shed used to be in one piece, with the truck parked inside."

"Is that so!" said the chief. "That's the strange thing about tornados. They can stay in a certain pathway where they destroy only what is directly in front of them and leave the rest intact."

"It seems it didn't even touch the house," said Dave.

"Good thing, too! Okay boys, which way to the cellar?" asked Chief Lomax. "Do you have your screwdriver with you, Jonathan?"

"Yes, sir," Jonathan said as he headed for the back of the house. He took the screwdriver out of his backpack and began to pry the door open. Just then, a faint "Meow" could be heard, and in a flash, the cat jumped up on the inside window sill.

"Well, there it is, just as you described it," said the chief. "It certainly does look like someone's pet, especially with that fancy collar. Dave, get Animal Rescue on the phone and see if they can come here. If they can catch it, they may be able to find out who owns it."

Jonathan went back to working on the cellar door and when it was opened, they all turned on their flashlights and climbed down the stairs, closing the door behind them. The cat stayed out of sight.

"It's this way." Jonathan headed for the back wall and slid the plywood aside. He squeezed through the opening and the others followed behind.

As they walked carefully through the tunnel, the chief paid close attention to the wire and lights. "You know, this certainly has a purpose. Someone needs it to do something illegal, I would think. We'll need to look into this further."

They continued on and the dirt floor of the tunnel became firm as they entered the cave. Jonathan kept the beam of his flashlight up high to the left, and soon the reflection from the neck chain sparkled in the darkness.

"Good night!" said the chief as he looked up at the gruesome sight. "Did you ever see anything like that before? That poor man."

"What a horrible way to die," Dave shook his head.

When Jonathan looked up, it seemed as if the head and feet were hanging even lower on either side of the spike than when he had seen it earlier that day.

Bright lights flashed as the deputy took photos from different angles.

"Here's where you can squeeze through to the ladder," Jonathan demonstrated.

Dave and Buzz followed between the two pillars, but Chief Lomax, who was a rather large man, had to twist his way through. "What a clever place to hide something," he said. "Who would ever think of bringing a ladder in here."

The deputy took more photographs. "Sir, would you like me to climb up and get some pictures of the chest and the body from that angle?"

"Sure, good idea, Dave," the chief stood, scratching his head. "That poor guy's plans are certainly shot."

"Would you like me to bring down the chest?" Dave asked.

"Yes, by all means," the Chief said. "There's no reason to leave it there. I'm going to get the coroner's office on the phone. I don't know how on earth they're going to get the body off that spike, but we'll see what they have to say." He worked his way back between the two pillars to make the call.

Soon he returned. "They're on their way. They're bringing an extra car to take you boys back to the station to get your bicycles. It's getting close to dinnertime and you'll need to get home. Thanks a lot for all your assistance." He smiled broadly. "I'll call you in a day or two."

Dave finished taking his photographs and climbed down the ladder, carrying the chest with him.

"We'll need to get that locked up in the evidence locker," said the chief. "Boys, would you like to meet the coroner at the front and show him the way back here? That would be very helpful."

"Yes, Sir," said Jonathan. He and Buzz hurried towards the tunnel.

They had just emerged outside into daylight, when two cars pulled up the lane. The first one, a large black van, had the coroner's government seal on the door. The smaller car belonged to an assistant. As both men got out, Jonathan approached them. "Chief Lomax asked us to show you where the body is."

"Oh, that's great. Thanks a lot, boys," said the coroner. Both men followed Jonathan and Buzz through the house and tunnel and into the cave where the chief stood waiting. They shook hands.

"Thanks again for all your help, boys," said Chief Lomax. "I'll give you a call soon. When word of this gets out, I imagine a reporter from the Woodland Chronicle will want to interview you."

The coroner's assistant then escorted Jonathan and Buzz back to his car and drove them to the police station.

As they got on their bikes, Buzz looked worried. "I wonder what my parents are going to say when I get home. After they lecture me, I think Dad might think that we're like heroes for finding that poor guy."

"I'm not sure what my mom will say. I'm glad that Chief Lomax has already called them about what we reported," Jonathan said. "That makes it a lot easier."

"How are we going to explain going into the cave, and all that weird stuff?"

Jonathan thought for a moment. "You know, Buzz, I don't think we have to mention the trips to the cave or anything about what we saw. That's not part of this police investigation. The only thing our parents and the police need to know about is the entrance from the house to the body. We can't even show them where we entered the cave, because you can't get in now."

"Yeah, that's right," Buzz looked relieved. "And anyway, it would be impossible to explain what went on in there. Nobody would believe us."

"You're not kidding. They'd want to take us to see a shrink," Jonathan sighed. "I'll call you tonight."

They took off on their bikes for home.

# CHAPTER 12

## AN OMINOUS THREAT

The next morning, Jonathan put on the television and sat down to eat breakfast. He turned to the local channel in time to see a reporter from the <u>Woodland Chronicle</u> standing at the end of the lane leading to the old house. A yellow CAUTION tape encircled the property to keep the curious out, including the reporter. Jonathan raced to the phone to call Buzz.

"Buzz, turn on the TV. The local station is reporting on the old house. I'll call you later." He hurried back to the living room just as the reporter began to speak:

*Last night, the coroner's office issued a statement regarding the removal of a body from inside a cave located in the Great National Forest. The cave appears to be connected to this house. The police are awaiting the outcome of an autopsy to find the exact cause of death and the report from forensics to identify the victim.*

\* \* \*

Five days later, Jonathan received a phone call from Chief Lomax requesting that he and Buzz come down to the station for an update.

When they arrived, they were ushered into the chief's office.

"Hello, boys," he smiled. "How are you doing?"

"Fine, thanks, Sir," they said in unison.

"Please have a seat."

They both sat down.

"I thought you would be interested in the information we've discovered since I last saw you. A reporter from the Woodland Chronicle will join us shortly. He wants to run the story for tomorrow's edition, including a photo of the two of you. Forensics has identified the victim by his fingerprints. His name is Arthur Fleetwood. He's been in and out of prison for petty theft and robbery for several years. He frequently moved about within the country, and the police have been unable to locate any next-of-kin."

Jonathan asked, "Did the police find anything else inside the house?"

"No," the chief replied. "There were some dirty clothes and a couple of boxes of cereal, but that's all."

"Did they find the cat?" Buzz asked.

"No, they didn't. It's probably hiding somewhere in the cave. We contacted Animal Rescue, and they said they would set a trap with some food in an attempt to catch it. Then it can go to a foster home to await possible adoption."

"Maybe Mom and I can adopt it," Jonathan said. "That'd be so cool. But I'd have to ask her first."

"I'll certainly notify them of that, Jonathan, as soon as I find out the status of their attempt. By the way, you'll be interested to know we took the jewelry chest to Robinson's jewelry store for identification. The owner recognized several pieces at once. I had hoped that case would be solved by now, but the owner reminded us that there had been two robbers. One served as the lookout while the other suggested he had a gun, but he never showed it. A car was parked around the corner and they got away before anyone realized what had happened. At the time, he had been so frightened, he was able to remember the whole experience as clearly as if it was yesterday."

Just then, the reporter arrived.

"Come in, Jack," Chief Lomax stood up. "I would like you to meet our two amateur detectives who discovered the victim, Jonathan Taylor and Buzz Cameron."

"Hello, boys," Jack said. "I'm delighted to meet you. You certainly helped make my work easier, and much more interesting for the public." He gave each of them a handshake. "I would like to get a photo of you both with Chief Lomax. Right here in the office would be fine."

"They stood up together in front of the mahogany desk and the camera flashed. "This will be in tomorrow's paper." Jack smiled. "You're famous!"

"Thanks again, boys," said the chief. "If anything else about this case crops up that I think you'd be interested in, I'll give you a call. Now, I'll need to go over some of the events with Jack for his report."

"Good bye Chief Lomax, and thank you," Jonathan said and they headed for home.

The next day, Jonathan tore down the street on his bicycle to the store to buy a copy of the morning edition of the Woodland Chronicle. The picture was on the front page, in color, with their names underneath and the caption:

*Two local boys discover a body in a cave located on the Jacobsville side of the Great National Forest. Apparently, a tunnel had been dug to join the cave to an isolated house off the main road. The victim, Arthur Fleetwood, age 53, has no known next-of-kin. Although the death appears to be accidental, an investigation is ongoing.*

Jonathan bought two copies, just in case Buzz's family hadn't seen it yet. He hurried over to their house and rang the doorbell.

Buzz's mother opened the door. "Hi, Jonathan," she said. "We're just going to have breakfast. Come, sit down and join us."

"I brought today's newspaper to show you our picture. See, it's right on the front page, in color, too." He handed it to her.

"Oh my, that's a very good picture," she smiled.

"Wow!" Buzz said as he looked over her shoulder. "We're like the main story." Then he quickly read the article. "That poor guy. Probably nobody even cares that he's dead."

"We'll have to show that to your dad when he comes home from work." She mixed up some scrambled eggs and poured them into a pan to cook. Then she put several slices of bread into the toaster oven.

"He was very concerned when Chief Lomax called to report what you boys had been up to. Thank goodness the whole thing is over and you're both safe." She put the eggs and toast on the table, poured orange juice into three glasses, and they sat down.

When they had finished eating, as they were helping to clear the table, Buzz said, "Jonny, want to go bike riding or something?"

"Sure," Jonathan answered. "Let's go over to my house and shoot baskets."

"Okay. We haven't done that for a while." They headed toward the door.

"Thanks a lot for breakfast, Mrs. Cameron," Jonathan said. "It was really good." They rode off on their bikes.

Jonathan got the basketball from inside the garage and they began to play one-on-one at the hoop that stood just outside the door. Within a short time, they began to get hot in the bright sunshine.

"I wonder if the yellow CAUTION tape is still there," Jonathan said.

"Let's go and find out." Buzz set the ball down.

"Okay," Jonathan nodded. "Even though the investigation is ongoing, I'll bet they're finished with examining the house. But we won't try to go inside anyway."

They got on their bikes and took off down the road. When they reached the lane leading to the house, the yellow tape was still in place.

"If we go through the woods toward the house on the outside of the tape, we won't be breaking the law," Jonathan said. They pushed their bikes up the incline into the woods along the side of the house, then hid them behind a dense thicket and continued walking up.

Suddenly, a car came tearing up the lane at a high rate of speed, spinning its wheels and breaking the tape. Jonathan and Buzz crouched down behind a bush to watch. The car stopped in front of the house and a short man with long, black, greasy hair and a bushy mustache got out and went around to the back. The car was a very old model, faded blue. The left front headlight and fender were smashed in, and the left front hubcap was missing. With the man out of sight, Jonathan tried to position himself to see the rear license plate, but it was so dirty he could not read the numbers. But he did notice it looked white with a blue stripe around the edge. Soon the man emerged carrying a large box with 'RCA Television' on the side. He put it on the rear seat of the car and went back inside the house.

"Where did he find that?" Jonathan asked.

"Maybe it was in the upstairs of the house," Buzz said. "We never went up there."

"But the chief said the police looked all around inside. That's so weird." Jonathan shook his head.

Soon the man returned, this time carrying a box labeled 'IBM Computer.' He put it in the trunk. He was getting ready to enter the car, when he seemed to sense being watched. As he turned to look, Jonathan and Buzz ducked back out of sight.

"That was close," Jonathan said as the car turned and sped down the lane.

"I hope he didn't see us." Buzz sounded worried. "If we were able to see him, he could probably see us."

"He'd just think we were two kids hanging out," Jonathan said. "I guess maybe we'd better go home."

"Yeah," Buzz agreed. "I'm supposed to help Dad at the garage today. I'll take the newspaper with me and see what he says about it."

When Jonathan arrived home, he made a sandwich and sat in front of the television to eat. He had just turned it on, when the phone rang. Not wanting to be disturbed, he lifted the receiver, then turned on the speakerphone. A gruff voice on the other end asked, "Jonathan Taylor?"

"Yes, it is," he answered. "Who's speaking?"

"Well now, that would be none of your business," said the voice. "I saw your picture in the newspaper, and this morning I saw you and your little friend trying to hide behind the bushes. You'd better stay away from that house if ya know what's good for ya. It was easy to find your phone number, and now I know where you live. Nobody messes with me. I could snap your neck like a twig, and I wouldn't think twice about doing it. Do you get it, kid?"

Jonathan, who by this time, was sitting straight up on the edge of the sofa, could hardly speak. But he managed to say, in a cracked voice, "Yes, Sir, I sure do."

"Call the cops, and you're dead meat." He hung up.

# CHAPTER 13

## AN ESCAPE PLAN

When Jonathan's mother arrived home later that afternoon, he was sitting in the living room staring into space.

"Hi, Dear," she said. "I'll start dinner in a minute. I just have to unwind first." She sat down. "Oh, by the way, one of the girls at work showed everybody the newspaper with the picture of you and Buzz. She kept referring to you as the local detectives." His mother kicked off her shoes. "I stopped at the grocery store and bumped into Molly Bender. Do you know she's still driving her car? Remember when she rammed into that chicken truck. I thought she might have lost her license, but apparently not. She must be in her 90's by now."

Jonathan sat stone-faced and couldn't reply.

"Is anything wrong, Dear?" his mother asked. "You're so quiet."

"Yes, Mom. Something happened today."

"For goodness sake, what?" she asked with an expression of alarm on her face.

"It's about the body that Buzz and I found in the cave, and about the police discovering he was the one who robbed the jewelry store a while ago."

"You mean there's more? I don't know how much more I can take. Chief Lomax told me all about it, and with the story in the newspaper, I thought the case was closed."

"Well, it turns out there were two robbers. The other one must have driven the getaway car. Apparently, he saw the article in the paper with our pictures and our names. I guess he didn't know where the other robber went, until he saw the newspaper and read that we found him dead in the cave. He must have thought the guy had skipped town with the jewelry."

"For goodness sake, Jonathan! What are you getting at?" she asked in a high pitched voice.

"Well, Buzz and I rode by the old house this afternoon, just to see if the yellow CAUTION tape was still up, and we saw this guy in a car break through the tape and come tearing up the driveway. He went into the house. In a few minutes, he came out with a new television and a computer, still in their boxes. We were hiding behind the bushes, but I think he saw us, because I had just got home when he phoned here. He said he saw my picture in the newspaper and now he knows where I live, and if I tell the cops about seeing him, I'll be dead meat."

"What!" His mother jumped up. "You've put both of us into a very dangerous situation. I have no choice here. I've got to call the police and report this."

"But he said he would kill me." Jonathan's lower lip quivered as tears began to run down his cheeks.

"No, he won't," she assured him. "The police will know what to do." She went straight to the phone. Jonathan followed her.

"May I speak to Chief Lomax, please? This is Jean Taylor, Jonathan's mother. It's urgent!" When the chief answered, she explained in a quavering voice what Jonathan had just told her. Her hand was shaking when she finally hung up. "The chief will be right over."

Within 15 minutes, he pulled into the driveway in an unmarked car. He had changed to his off-duty clothes so as not to be recognized by anyone passing by, as he had no idea who or where the caller was.

Jonathan's mother opened the door, with Jonathan standing behind her.

"Chief Lomax, I'm so glad to see you," she said as she shook his hand. "Jonathan and I are quite alarmed about that threatening phone call. Please come in."

The chief followed her into the living room and sat down. "Jonathan, I am so sorry you're being put into the middle of this and were threatened by this man. Unfortunately, the thief and his accomplice just disappeared after robbing the jewelry store. We thought they had probably fled the area. No one was ever able to see what they looked like because of their masks, or find fingerprints or clues as to their identity. When you found the stolen jewelry along with the dead body, we still had no idea who the accomplice had been, or even if he was still alive. It's been three years since the robbery. I guess the article in the paper made him aware of the existence of the rest of the stolen property and felt it belonged to him, until you and Buzz came on the scene."

Jonathan's mother gasped, "I'm terribly afraid of what this man could do to us if he knew we had contacted you."

"I can certainly understand that," Chief Lomax said. "We don't want him to know you reported this. I'll get in touch with the editor of the newspaper to see if he can run a column about the case on the front page in tomorrow's early edition, suggesting there are no new leads. Hopefully, he'll see it because, apparently, he read yesterday's paper."

"He must be staying somewhere near Jacobsville," Jonathan's mother suggested. "That's a very scary thought."

"You're right," said the chief. "That's why we need to start arranging for you two to get out of town."

"What about Buzz?" asked Jonathan.

"I checked with Buzz's family, and the suspect has not contacted them. But just to be safe, the head mechanic at his father's garage invited them to stay with his family until we catch this guy. Meanwhile, Mrs. Taylor, do you have any relatives or friends where you and Jonathan could stay for a day or two, if necessary?"

"My sister, Betty, lives on a farm just outside of town. We could stay there."

"I think that would be a good idea," the chief nodded. "It would at least give you peace of mind, even if you're not in danger. You would still be able to go to work from there, and you'll know Jonathan will be safe because that man will have no idea where he is. Meanwhile, Jonathan, I would like a description of the vehicle the man was driving, with as much detail as you can possibly give me." He took a pad and pen out of his pocket.

Jonathan sat up very straight in his seat to concentrate on picturing the car. "Well, Sir, the car was quite old and faded blue. It had four doors. I remember that because he put one of the boxes in the back seat. The front left headlight and fender were smashed in, and the left front hubcap was missing. It looked as if it had been in an accident. I tried to see the license plate on the back bumper, but it was so dirty I couldn't read the numbers. I think it was white, but the edges looked blue."

"Jonathan, you're very observant. That description will be quite helpful. I wouldn't be surprised if that plate with the blue edging was from Minnesota," the chief smiled. "Did you manage to get a good look at the man?"

"Yes, pretty good," Jonathan said. "He was short, with long, black, greasy hair and a bushy mustache. He wore an orange colored T-shirt with the picture of a big sun on the back."

"Excellent job, Jonathan," said the chief. "As soon as I get back to my office, I'm going to compile your information for an APB, that means an all points bulletin, to be sent out immediately to alert people to be on the lookout for this man.

I think it shouldn't be too difficult to find him, especially with your description of the license plate. This is a very small town. Most people know everybody and would certainly be aware of a stranger. I called Deputy Dave Adam just before I got here, asking him to come so I can go back to the station and get right on this. He'll bring his own car to prevent suspicion. He should be here in a few minutes, and he can stay until you and Jonathan leave."

"Thank you. I really appreciate that." Jonathan's mother got up and went to the kitchen to phone her sister.

"Jonathan, I think the robber's threat is just something to keep you quiet," Chief Lomax said. "I can't imagine him wasting precious time coming here to get even with you. He'll want to get out of town with the stolen goods as soon as possible."

"I hope so," Jonathan said. "But I'm glad we'll be going to Uncle Bill and Aunt Betty's place anyway. My cousin Melissa lives there too."

"Well, it sounds as if you'll have a good time."

Just then, the deputy arrived, and Chief Lomax stood up to let him in.

"Mrs. Taylor, this is my deputy, Dave Adam." They shook hands.

"Thank you for coming," she said. "I'll start packing right now."

"May I have your sister's phone number?" the chief asked. "I'll contact you as soon as I know more of what's going on. We'll be checking all the nearby motels and any other likely places where the suspect might be staying. I'll put another deputy at the old house, in case he comes back for more of the stolen goods. We already searched the place quite thoroughly and found nothing. I can't imagine where he's been hiding the stuff."

Chief Lomax headed for the door. "Dave, after Jonathan and his mother have left, be sure the house is locked up tight, then come back to the station. I have another couple of places for you to check out."

# CHAPTER 14

## Sanctuary on the Farm

When Jonathan and his mother approached the entrance to Uncle Bill's farm, Melissa, who was sitting on a large rock adjusting her long, blond ponytail, stood up and waved. As the car stopped, she hurried over and Jonathan jumped out and shut the door. They ran up the lane together. Jonathan's mother followed in the car. When she reached the farmhouse, she got out, and Betty came running outside to give her a big hug.

"Jeanie, I'm so glad you're here," she said. "When you called, I was very frightened for you. That man sounds like a desperate criminal."

"You're right. When Jonathan told me about that phone call I was so frightened. But, after speaking with the police chief, I feel much better. Thank goodness you live so close, or I don't know what we'd do."

"Come inside," Betty said. "I started dinner as soon as you phoned."

As Jonathan and Melissa continued up the lane, they passed the herd of black and white Holstein cows eating grass on the other side of the split rail fence. Several of them raised their heads to watch as they walked by, then resumed eating.

"Look over there," Melissa pointed to a black and white calf standing beside its mother as she grazed. "He was so cute when he was born, but he's getting a lot bigger now. I call him Morty. Oh, and we got two new horses too, about three weeks ago. Dad bought them at an auction."

They reached the red barn, with its large, open doorway and went inside.

"Can you ride the horses?" Jonathan asked.

"Sure, you and I could go riding, if you like. I'll ask my dad. He'll be home soon." Melissa was so thrilled to have her cousin visiting, she was practically jumping up and down.

"I don't know if I want to," Jonathan said. "I've only been on a horse once, and I didn't like it too much. Maybe you could show me how. I think the horse I rode knew I didn't know what I was doing, and he didn't think that was very cool."

"Dad taught me on Susie about five years ago," Melissa said. "It wasn't really that hard once I learned how to handle her. But Susie's getting older now. You can still ride her, just not too long, or too hard. So now I have Bessie." She stopped in front of a stall where one of the horses stuck his head out. "I named this one Artie," she stroked his nose. "Do like this," she demonstrated. "He likes it."

Jonathan worked up his courage and followed her example. "You're right. I think he does like it," he smiled, feeling a little more confident.

"Bess is the one in this next stall," Melissa said as she moved over. "You're the one I like to ride, isn't that right, Bessie?" The horse came right to her to be petted. "These two are both, like, real gentle."

Then, Melissa went to the end stall where Susie was busy eating from her feed bucket.

"Hello, Susie," she said. "Come here, Sweetie."

The horse took her nose out of the bucket, paused, then walked toward Melissa.

"That's my good girl." Melissa reached out, patted her neck and stroked her mane. "See what a nice girl she is."

"Okay, I think I'd like to learn how to ride," Jonathan said. "Once you get up close to the horses, they're awesome. It would be such fun if we could go riding together."

"How long do you think you'll be able to stay here?" Melissa asked.

"I guess until the police catch that guy and it's safe to go home."

"I saw the picture of you and Buzz in the newspaper. I guess everybody in town sees you two as the local celebrities," she laughed.

"I don't know about that," Jonathan said. "Buzz and I just happened to be exploring in the cave, and there the guy was, hanging on that spike. By the look of him, I think he'd been there for quite a while."

"Eewww, seriously?" she curled her lower lip. "What did he look like?"

"Well, when I climbed up the ladder and looked down, there he was right in front of my face."

"Was he all funny-looking?" Melissa screwed up her face in disgust.

"Yeah, you could say that. You'd never see anybody like that walking around on the street, unless he was a zombie." He grinned. "His eyes and cheeks were sort of sunk in, like, dried up."

"Yuck. That's so disgusting," she shivered. "I'm glad I didn't see it. I would have had nightmares for a month."

"Yeah, I know what you mean. I didn't have any yet, but I still could, because I keep thinking about that face." Jonathan said.

"Do you believe that guy would really have come after you for telling the police?" she asked.

"I don't know. He sounded so scary, I was totally freaked out. But Mom called them anyway. Chief Lomax said the guy probably wouldn't want to waste time coming after me. He'd want to hurry up and get all the loot he stored in the house or cave, wherever he hid it, and get out of town."

Just then, Uncle Bill rode up in a pickup truck, with his black and white shaggy dog sitting beside him. He stopped in front of the barn and they both got out. Melissa called to the dog, "Come, Bear." She clapped her hands. "Here, boy." The dog came running, wagging his tail. She rubbed his head. "Did you have fun in the field?"

Uncle Bill kicked one of the tires to get the mud off his boots, then he went straight over to Jonathan. "Hi there, Buddy," he said giving him a high-five. "I'm glad to see you and that you're safe. What a frightening thing it must have been to be threatened like that."

"Yeah, it sure was," Jonathan said. "At least I don't have to worry now. He'd never be able to find me here."

"Well, you can stay with us as long as you need to. Betty and I always enjoy having you and your mom come to visit. I know your mom works so hard, it's difficult for her to come over. With the shifts and all, she's probably tired a lot of the time. I know Melissa wishes you were here more often." He smiled at his daughter. "You two are like twins. You're the same age and you get along so well."

"Dad, could you teach Jonathan how to ride Arty?" Melissa asked. "Then he and I could ride around the farm. It would be lots of fun."

"Sure, I'd like to do that, but not in the next few days," he said. "I have an awful lot of work to do now that Mike, my hired hand, is out sick. Anyway, it would take a couple of weeks or so to teach you, Jonathan. There are things you need to learn about horses so you can understand them. Even though they're so big, they're very sensitive animals. You can't just jump on a horse and take off like riding a motorcycle. It needs a lot of care. Before and after riding, you must check its hooves and, using a hoof pick, remove any small stones or other material from the stall trapped underneath, so the horse won't go lame. Mike will show you how to lift up the horse's foot."

"They're used to having this done," said Melissa.

"That's right, Honey," Uncle Bill said. "You also need to learn how to gently brush its body, then its mane and tail after riding."

"This is going to be really fun," Jonathan grinned.

"I think you will find it a real bonding experience," said Uncle Bill. "You'll become very comfortable around these animals."

"You can give the horse an apple to eat," said Melissa. "They really like that."

"Arty's very calm and a good boy to ride while you're learning and getting comfortable with him," Uncle Bill said. "But I'll need to run it by your mom first. Let's go and see if dinner's ready. It's about that time." He started to walk toward the house, with Bear running along beside him.

Jonathan watched Uncle Bill as he walked ahead, with a feeling of longing. Uncle Bill reminded him of his own father who left right after his sixth birthday to look for work, but he never came back.

"You know, Melissa, you're so lucky to have such a nice dad. When I see him, I wish my dad was still here. I wonder if he would have liked to go horseback riding with me, or fishing in the forest." A sad look crossed his face.

"He might have," Melissa said. "Maybe some day he'll come back looking for you and you can tell him about all the fun things he missed."

"Yeah, that's true." Jonathan's spirits seemed to brighten up. "He really might come back."

As they approached the house they could smell the aroma of freshly baked bread in the air.

"You're just in time," said Aunt Betty as they entered the kitchen. "When you've finished washing your hands, we'll have everything on the table."

Jonathan and Melissa came into the dining room and sat down beside each other. Platters had been set in the middle of the table loaded with mashed potatoes, chicken cutlets, green beans and a large, tossed salad. There was a basket full of rolls, still warm from the oven.

"Be sure to leave room for dessert," said Aunt Betty. "I baked an apple pie."

Just as the dessert was being served, Uncle Bill looked over at Jonathan's mother. "Jeanie, what do you think of Jonathan learning to ride one of our horses?"

She thought for a moment then smiled at Jonathan. "It's up to him. I think it might be a good experience."

"I know how hard your job is," Uncle Bill said. "Those shifts and weekends can be exhausting. And it's such a challenge keeping kids busy in the summertime. I was just thinking, I could drive over to your place from time to time and bring Jonathan back here and teach him to ride. He and Melissa would have such a good time."

"That would be wonderful," she said.

"Could Buzz come sometimes, too?" Melissa asked.

"Sure, in fact, I could pick him up at the same time, if his parents agree. I know you and Buzz are best friends, Jonathan. But we'll need to get their permission first."

"It'd be so much fun," Melissa smiled.

"Yeah, that'd be real cool," Jonathan said with a big smile on his face. "I can hardly wait."

When dinner was over, everybody helped clear the table. Uncle Bill went outside to the barn and Jonathan and Melissa sat down in front of the television in the living room. Melissa turned on the local station for any news of the police investigation. A food channel program was just finishing, when it was interrupted by a special report. An artist's sketch of the vehicle Jonathan had described to the police was on the screen, along with the likeness of the driver. A reporter came on the scene:

*Police are looking for an unidentified male who resembles the description of this artist's sketch. He was last seen driving an old blue four-door sedan with left front damage as shown on the illustration. The license plate is white and edged in blue. This man is wanted for questioning about a robbery in Robinson's jewelry store three years ago. Anyone with information regarding this case is requested to please contact the Jacobsville Police Department immediately.*

"Mom," Jonathan got up and ran to the kitchen. "Melissa and I just saw an announcement about the guy they're looking for." His mother and Aunt Betty hurried to the living room, but the announcement was over.

"The sketches by the artist were really good," Jonathan said. "They looked just like the guy."

"I'm glad they're getting right on it," his mother said. "I think it won't be too hard to find him with that old wreck he's driving, unless he changes cars."

# CHAPTER 15

## MYSTERY SOLVED

The next morning Jonathan was awakened by a rooster crowing so loudly it seemed to be right underneath his window. He got up to look outside. The brightly colored bird, with a red comb on the top of his head, was strutting around between the house and a chicken coop just beyond the back yard. There, several hens were busy clucking and pecking at the corn mash that had been scattered outside.

Jonathan could hear voices coming from the kitchen. He got dressed and went downstairs. Melissa was sitting in front of the TV while Jonathan's mother helped Aunt Betty prepare breakfast.

"Did you sleep okay?" Melissa asked.

"Yes, I sure did. I went right out."

"So did I," she said. "Dad was already gone when I got up. He went to check out a fence that needs mending."

"Breakfast is ready," Aunt Betty announced.

Melissa turned off the TV, and they both went to the dining room and sat at the table. In the center, a plate piled with pancakes sat next to a platter of poached eggs and bacon that gave off a mouth-watering aroma.

"Help yourselves," Aunt Betty said, and she sat down. "Bill left right after breakfast. He has a lot of work to do. It's too much for just one person. I hope Mike's feeling better soon."

"What are you two going to do today?" asked Jonathan's mother.

"We could just hang out at the barn," Melissa said. "Or, has anyone gone to collect the eggs today?"

"No, not yet," Aunt Betty said. "That would be a big help."

As soon as they had finished eating, Melissa and Jonathan cleared their dishes from the table and put them in the dishwasher.

Just then the phone rang. Melissa answered. "She's right here. Aunt Jean, it's for you."

"Hello, Chief Lomax," Jonathan's mother said and listened for a few minutes. "We'll see you later." She hung up the phone with a big smile on her face. "They got him." She gave a huge sigh of relief.

"Yes-s-s!" Jonathan shouted as he pumped his fist in the air.

"The chief said that a couple of young hikers noticed the blue car parked behind an old barn and recognized it from the sketch on television that was drawn from Jonathan's description."

"Yea!" Jonathan shouted.

She continued. "They crouched down when a man came out and got into the car, then drove away. They went into the barn and it looked as if that's where he had spent the night. They called the police."

"How did the police catch him?" asked Jonathan.

"Apparently, he went back to the old house to collect more of the stolen goods, and the deputy who was on duty there called it in."

"Well, that certainly didn't take long," Aunt Betty said.

"You're right. Chief Lomax said it's safe to come home now. He asked if you and Buzz could come to headquarters for a lineup to positively identify the man. They need your testimony that the man you saw carrying the boxes out of the house is the same one they arrested. They want to make sure he isn't part of a larger operation, with more individuals involved than they're aware of. He has already spoken with Buzz's mother."

"Did he say where they had hidden the boxes at the house?" Jonathan asked.

"No, he didn't," she said. "He'll give us all the details when we go down there."

"How soon can we go?" asked Jonathan.

"We're supposed to be there around 10 o'clock, so they can get on with the investigation."

"Should we pick up Buzz and take him with us?" asked Jonathan.

"I was just thinking that would be a good idea, because we'll be driving right past his house anyway. I'll give his mother a call." She soon returned.

"Buzz's mother was very grateful that we could pick him up. She's expecting several workmen to come and do repairs on their house. They're so booked up she didn't want to have to cancel them. I told her we'd be there in one hour."

"I'd better get ready," Jonathan started upstairs to get his backpack. "I'll call you and tell you all about it, Melissa, just as soon as we're finished."

Jonathan and his mother left the house and headed for their car with Aunt Betty and Melissa walking behind.

"I wish you two could stay longer, Jeanie," Aunt Betty said as she gave her sister a big hug. "Call me and let me know what happens."

"Thanks a lot, Aunt Betty," Jonathan said. "I'll see you both real soon."

When they arrived at Buzz's house, two trucks were parked in the driveway. Buzz, who had been sitting on the steps waiting, stood up, raced to the car and got in.

"This should be so cool," he said. "I've never seen a lineup before."

"Neither have I. Only on TV," Jonathan said. "What if they all look alike?"

"What if they put identical twins up to fool us?" Buzz said.

"That guy could never be a twin. No other person in this world could look like him," Jonathan laughed.

When they arrived at the police station, Sergeant Graham got up from his desk. "Hello, Mrs. Taylor, boys. Please follow me." He led them into Chief Lomax's office and closed the door.

The chief stood up. "Thank you for coming so promptly. Please sit down."

After they had settled themselves in the polished mahogany chairs, Chief Lomax began.

"The other men in the lineup haven't arrived yet. I'm expecting them momentarily. Meanwhile, there's been an interesting development at the old house. After the man was picked up there, the deputy who was on duty went through the tunnel. When he came to the end, he noticed a mark on the ground that looked like scraping in front of one of those huge rocks at the side. He braced himself against it to bend over and examine the mark more closely, and as he did so he felt the rock move slightly. He stood up and pushed it. To his amazement, it was perfectly balanced. It spun around and opened up a large space behind. Apparently, the wiring on the side of the tunnel had been carefully tucked around the opening and continued on into that empty space. When he shone his flashlight into the darkness, it illuminated stacks of boxes containing electronics."

"That's were they hid the stuff," Jonathan said in an excited voice.

"We never saw that," Buzz looked over at Jonathan.

"It was very cleverly concealed," Chief Lomax said. "The man we have in custody was just released from prison two weeks ago, where he had spent time for another robbery he committed shortly after the jewelry store heist. He probably thought his partner had already taken off with the goods while he was in jail. But when he saw the newspaper article and photo, he realized the stolen goods were still hidden in the tunnel."

Just then, there was a knock on the door. Sergeant Graham announced, "The three men for the lineup have arrived."

"Thank you," said the chief. "We'll be right there."

While Sergeant Graham led the men to the lineup room, and retrieved the prisoner from his cell, Chief Lomax took Jonathan, first, into a darkened room with a large one-way window. The men stood in a line with numbers from one to four on the wall above their heads.

"Jonathan, do you recognize anyone there?"

"Yes, number two," Jonathan said with no hesitation. "I remember his bushy mustache and that long, black, greasy hair. And he's shorter than the other men. That's him, alright."

"Thank you, Jonathan. Now I'll take you back and bring in Buzz and see what he remembers."

In a few minutes, Buzz emerged from the dark room. "He was easy to spot."

"Thank you for your help, boys," the chief said. "I called the reporter from the Woodland Chronicle and he'll be preparing his story for tomorrow morning's paper."

"Chief Lomax," Jonathan asked, "Do you know if the Animal Rescue still has the cat from the house?"

"I don't know," he said. "Let's see. They said they would hold it until I called." He picked up the phone.

"What's this about a cat?" asked Jonathan's mother.

"Mom, it's so beautiful, and loves to be petted, and it has a blue collar on with a silver bell. Can we get it, please?"

The chief hung up the phone. "The cat is still there. It's a girl, by the way. You can pick her up if you like. What do you say, Mrs. Taylor?"

"I think a cat would be a wonderful addition to our home. I'm off work tomorrow, Jonathan. We can go to the pet shop and get everything we need."

Chief Lomax wrote down the address of the shelter along with the phone number and handed it to Jonathan.

As they left the Police Station, Jonathan's mother had a big smile on her face. "Are you boys hungry yet? It's nearly lunch time."

"I'm starving," said Jonathan.

"Me too," added Buzz.

"How about the Grill?" she asked.

"Sounds great," both boys said together.

The next morning, Jonathan hopped on his bike and hurried downtown to the Quik Mart to buy two newspapers, one for himself, and one for Buzz. Before returning home, he leafed through the paper. In the Local section, a two-column article described the capture of Joseph Reilly, a 35 year-old felon who, along with his accomplice, the late Arthur Fleetwood, age 53, were responsible for the robbery of Robinson's jewelry store in Jacobsville three years ago. It said:

*Jonathan Taylor and Buzz Cameron, who discovered the body of Mr. Fleetwood in the cave last week, identified Mr. Reilly in a lineup. He remains in jail awaiting sentencing.*

The story went on to describe the series of events that led to his arrest.

Jonathan pedaled his bike home as fast as he could to show the paper to his mother. Then he hurried over to Buzz's house. Buzz and his mother both came out to read it.

"I don't know what the Jacobsville police department would do without you two," she said.

Jonathan laughed. "We're the local detectives for hire."

"I'm not so sure about that." She laughed. "Summer vacation will soon be over and you two will have your work cut out for you."

"I guess I'd better get going," said Jonathan. "I have a lot to do today. Mom's off work, and we're going to the Animal Rescue to adopt the cat we found in the cave. I can hardly wait. I think I'll call her Tinkerbell."

He hopped on his bike, and took off for home.

## ABOUT THE AUTHOR

Sheila Adam McIntyre was born in Toronto, Canada and grew up in St. Jacobs, Ontario, a quaint little village surrounded by farm country. That simple life style is the inspiration for the small town atmosphere in this story.

After retiring from her career as a healthcare professional, she was able to pursue her favorite hobby, writing. Raising her three sons provided the opportunity to observe their natural curiosity and sense of adventure. She lives in New Jersey.

## Another Book by this Author

THE SECRET IN THE FOREST